Judy Moody
Predicts the Future

Alia Irizarry Ortiz

MW01042056

Books by Megan McDonald and Peter H. Reynolds:

#1 – *Judy Moody*

#2 – *Judy Moody Gets Famous!*

#3 – *Judy Moody Saves the World!*

#4 – *Judy Moody Predicts the Future*

#5 – *Judy Moody, M.D.: The Doctor Is In!*

#6 – *Judy Moody Declares Independence*

#7 – *Judy Moody Around the World in 8½ Days*

#1 – *Stink: The Incredible Shrinking Kid*

#2 – *Stink and the Incredible Super-Galactic Jawbreaker*

The Judy Moody Mood Journal

Judy Moody's Double-Rare Way-Not-Boring Book of Fun Stuff to Do

Books by Megan McDonald:

Ant and Honey Bee: What a Pair!

The Sisters Club

Books by Peter H. Reynolds:

The Dot

Ish

Judy Moody
Predicts the Future

Megan McDonald

illustrated by
Peter H. Reynolds

CANDLEWICK PRESS
CAMBRIDGE, MASSACHUSETTS

First paperback edition in this format 2006

The Library of Congress has cataloged the hardcover edition as follows:

McDonald, Megan.
Judy Moody predicts the future / Megan McDonald ;
illustrated by Peter H. Reynolds. —1st ed.
p. cm.
Summary: After Judy obtains a mood ring, she tries to convince herself
and her third-grade classmates that she can predict the future.
ISBN-13: 978-0-7636-1792-9 (hardcover)
ISBN-10: 0-7636-1792-X (hardcover)
[1. Prophecies—Fiction. 2. Rings—Fiction. 3. Schools—Fiction.]
I. Reynolds, Peter, date, ill. II. Title.
PZ7.M1487 Jr 2003
[Fic]—dc21   2002067053

ISBN-13: 978-0-7636-2343-2 (paperback)
ISBN-10: 0-7636-2343-1 (paperback)

4 6 8 10 9 7 5 3

Printed in the United States of America

This book was typeset in Stone Informal.
The illustrations were done in watercolor, tea, and ink.

Candlewick Press
2067 Massachusetts Avenue
Cambridge, Massachusetts 02140

visit us at www.candlewick.com

For Barbara Mauk and all the
readers of Parkview Center School
M. M.
To Dawn Haley, Master of Time & Space
P. H. R.

Table of Contents

The Mood Ring 1

Eeny Meany Green Zucchini 13

Toady Calling 23

Madame M for Moody 39

The Sleeping Speller 57

Preposterous Hippopotamus . . . 69

Antarctica 78

The V.I.Q. 88

Operation True Love 102

Non-Fiction Prediction . . . 116

Purple Mountain Majesty 134

Judy

Madame M for Moody, a.k.a.
the Sleeping Speller.

Who's

Dad

Judy's father.
Spaghetti maker and
#1 driver to Fur & Fangs.

Mom

Judy's mother.
Fond of hairbrushing to avoid
T. rex hair.

Mouse

Judy's cat.
Very predictable—or is she?

Stink

Judy's mood-ring stealing,
Virginia-creepy little brother.

Who

Rocky

Judy's baloney-eating
best friend.

Ms. Tater

The Crayon Lady

Mr. Todd

Judy's teacher, a.k.a.
Mr. New Glasses.

Frank

Mood rings don't lie.
Is Judy's friend REALLY
in love with her?

Jessica

Queen Bee Jessica Finch.
Proud owner of Thomas
Jefferson sticker. Never
been to Antarctica.

The Mood Ring

Judy Moody ate one, two, three bowls of cereal. No prize. She poured four, five, six bowls of cereal. Nothing. Seven. Out fell the Mystery Prize. She ripped open the paper wrapper.

A ring! A silver ring with an oogley center. A mood ring! And a little piece of cardboard.

WHAT MOOD ARE YOU IN? it asked.

What mood are you in?

BLACK	Grouchy. impossible!
AMBER	Nervous. Tense
GREEN	Jealous. Envy.
Blue-Green	Relaxed calm
DARK BLUE	Unhappy. SAD
Light Blue	Happy. GLAD!
Purple	Joyful on Top of the World
RED	Romantic. in love!

OFFICIAL MOOD RING GUIDE — PLACE RING ON FINGER OR PRESS THUMB TO CENTER OF RING HOLD FOR 3 SECONDS " FIND OUT WHAT MOOD YOU'RE IN!"

Judy slid the ring onto her finger. She pressed her thumb to the oogley center. She squeezed her eyes tight. One one-thousand, two one-thousand, three one-thousand. She hoped the ring was purple. Purple was the best. Purple was *Joyful, On Top of the World.*

At last, she dared to look. Oh no! She couldn't believe her eyes. The ring was black. She knew what black meant, even without the directions. Black said *Grouchy, Impossible.* Black was for a bad, mad mood!

Maybe I counted wrong, thought Judy. She closed her eyes and pressed the ring again. She thought only good thoughts this time. Happy thoughts.

She thought about the time she and Rocky and Frank put a fake hand in the toilet to play a trick on Stink. She thought about the time she got a picture of her elbow in the newspaper. She thought about the time Class 3T collected enough bottles to plant trees in the rain forest. She thought of purple things. Socks and rocks and Popsicles.

Judy Moody opened her eyes.

She flunked! The ring was still black.

Could the mood ring be wrong? Judy did not think rings could lie. Especially rings with directions.

Judy froze her thumb on an ice cube and pressed the ring's center. Black.

She ran her thumb under hot water and pressed it again. Black, black, blacker than black. Not one teeny bit purple.

I guess I'm in a bad mood and don't even know it, thought Judy. *What could I be mad about?*

Judy Moody went looking for a bad mood.

She found her dad outside, planting fall flower bulbs.

"Dad," she said, "will you take me to Fur & Fangs?"

Judy hated when her dad was too busy to take her to the pet store. She could already feel the bad mood coming on.

"Sure," said Dad. "Just let me rinse my hands."

"Really?" asked Judy.

"Really."

"But you look really busy. And I have homework."

"It's okay," said Dad. "I'm about finished. I'll just wash my hands and we'll go."

"But what about my homework?"

"Do it after dinner," said Dad.

"Never mind," said Judy.

"Huh?" asked her dad.

Judy Moody went looking for an even better bad mood.

It really bugged her when her mom told her to brush her hair. So Judy took out her ponytails on purpose. Her hair stuck out in *T. rex* spikes. Her bangs fell over her eyes.

She found her mom reading in the pink chair.

"Hi, Mom."

Her mom smiled at her. "Hi, honey."

"Aren't you going to say anything?" Judy asked.

"Like what?"

"Like, 'Go brush your hair. Get your hair out of your eyes. Your hair looks like a *T. rex.*' Anything."

"It's from the ponytails, honey. It'll be fine after you wash it tonight."

"But what if somebody came to our house and knocked on the door right this very second?" Judy asked.

"Like who? Rocky?" asked Mom.

"No, like the president of the United States," Judy said.

"Tell the president you'll be right down. Then run upstairs and brush your hair."

It was no use. Judy Moody had to find Stink. If anybody could put her in a bad mood, Stink could. The baddest.

Upstairs, Judy barged right into Stink's room without knocking.

"Stink! Where's all my doctor stuff?"

"What doctor stuff? I don't have any."

"But you always have my doctor stuff."

"You told me to stop taking everything."

"Do you have to listen to everything I say?" asked Judy.

Judy glared at her ring. "This mood ring lies." She yanked it off and threw it into the trash.

Stink fished the ring out of the trash. "A mood ring? Cool!" He tried on the ring. It turned black. Bat-wing black.

"See?" said Judy. "Worthless!"

Stink pressed his thumb to the oogley

center. The ring turned green! Green as a turtle's neck. Green as a toad's belly.

Judy could not believe her eyes. "Let me see that," she said. It was green all right. "Stink, you can give me back my mood ring now."

"You threw it in the trash," Stink told her, waving his mood-ring hand in front of her. "It's mine now."

"Yuck! Green looks like pond scum."

"Does not!"

"Green means jealous. Green means green with envy. Green means you wish you were me."

"Why would I wish that? You don't have a mood ring," said Stink.

"C'mon, Stinker. I went through seven bowls of cereal for that ring. I gave up going to Fur & Fangs for that ring. I froze and burned myself for that ring."

"It's still mine," said Stink.

"ROAR!" said Judy.

Eeny Meany Green Zucchini

The next day, Judy was in a mood. The burnt-toast kind of bad mood. The kind that turns your mood ring b-l-a-c-k.

If only she could convince Stink that she had magic powers. A person with magic powers should own a mood ring. What good was a mood ring in the hands of someone with un-magic powers?

Where was that Stink-a-Roo anyway?

Probably down in the living room, reading the encyclopedia.

Judy ran downstairs. Stink was lying on the floor with encyclopedias all around him, wiggling his loose tooth.

"I knew it!" said Judy. "I just predicted you'd be reading the encyclopedia. I have special powers, superduper magic powers, see-the-future powers!"

"I'm always reading the encyclopedia," said Stink. "Which letter am I on?"

"*M,*" said Judy.

"WRONG!" said Stink. "*S!*"

"I still predicted it," said Judy. What else could she predict?

Judy went to the kitchen and brought back a Tasty Tuna Treat for Mouse.

She hid it in her pocket.

"I predict that Mouse will come into the room," she said. She waved the Tasty Tuna Treat behind her back, where Stink couldn't see it.

Mouse came slinking into the room. "Mouse!" said Judy. "What a surprise! Except . . . I predicted it! Ha!"

"Mouse always comes into the room we're in," said Stink.

"Well, what if I said I could read our mother's mind?"

"I'd rather read the encyclopedia," said Stink.

"Stink, you have to come with me!" said Judy. "So I can prove my amazing powers of prediction!" Stink followed Judy into Mom's office.

"Hi, Mom," said Judy. "Guess what?"

"What is it?" said Mom, looking up over her glasses.

"I know what you're thinking," said Judy. She squeezed her eyes shut, wrinkled her nose, and pressed her fingertips to her temples.

"You're thinking . . . you wish I'd clean under my bed for once instead of bugging you. You're thinking . . . you wish Stink would get his homework out of the way for the weekend."

"Amazing! That's exactly what I'm thinking!" said Mom.

"See?" said Judy.

"Were you really thinking that, Mom?" asked Stink.

"Now I predict that Dad will walk into the house," said Judy.

"You heard the garage door," said Stink.

"True. Okay, it's Dad's night to cook. I predict spaghetti."

"All he knows how to make is either spaghetti or ziti."

Stink ran into the kitchen. Judy ran after him.

"Dad, Dad!" Stink said. "What's for dinner?"

"Spaghetti," said Dad.

"Lucky guess," Stink said to Judy.

"ESP," Judy said.

"Okay," said Stink. "I'm thinking of a number."

"It doesn't work like that," said Judy.

"C'mon! What's the number?"

Judy grabbed a dishtowel and wrapped it around her head like a turban.

She closed her eyes. She pressed her fingertips to her temples. She made funny noises. "Ali baba, abra-ca-dab-ra. Eeny meany green zucchini."

"Does the dishtowel help with ESP?" asked Stink.

"Quiet! I'm concentrating."

"Hurry up. What am I thinking?"

"You're thinking I don't really have Extra Special Powers."

"Right," said Stink.

"You're thinking ESP shouldn't take this long," Judy said.

"Right! What about my number?"

Stink's favorite number was always his age. "Seven," said Judy.

"Right again!" said Stink. "Now I'm thinking of a color."

"Pond-scum green?" said Judy.

"Wrong! Eggplant," said Stink.

"EGGPLANT! Eggplant is not a color! Eggplant is not even an egg. Eggplant is a vegetable. A squeegy-weegy vegetable."

"I was still thinking it," said Stink. "You

have about as much magic power as an eggplant. A squeegy-weegy eggplant."

"Face it, Stink. I have special powers. Even without my mood ring."

"So you don't need it back," said Stink, flashing the ring under Judy's nose.

"A person with special powers, such as mine, should have a mood ring. It goes with predicting the future, like a crystal ball. Has the ring turned purple on you?"

"Nope."

"See? It only turns purple on Extra-Special-Powers people. It turns pond-scum green on plain old encyclopedia readers."

Stink stared at the ring.

"In fact, I predict that your finger will

turn green and fall off if you don't give me back my ring," said Judy.

"I'm never taking it off," said Stink.

"We'll see," said Judy.

Toady Calling

On Saturday, Stink was reading the encyclopedia. Again! He wiggled his loose tooth some more. With his mood-ring finger, of course. The mood ring glowed. It glittered. It gleamed. Stink scratched his head with his mood-ring finger about one hundred times a minute.

"Stink, do you have lice or something?" Judy asked.

"No," said Stink. "I have a mood ring!" He laughed himself silly.

Mr. Lice Head was giving Judy a bad case of the Moody blues. She could not stay in the same room and watch her mood-ring-that-wasn't-hers one more minute. She needed to think.

Judy looked out the back door. It was raining outside. She pulled on her rubber boots, dashed across the backyard, and crawled inside the Toad Pee Club Clubhouse (a.k.a. the old blue tent).

Plip-plop, plip-plop went the rain. It was lonely in the clubhouse all by herself. She wished the other members of the Toad Pee Club were here. Well, at least Rocky and Frank Pearl, not Stink.

She even missed Toady. Maybe she shouldn't have let Toady go after all. Even if it was to help save the world.

Ra-reek! Ra-reek! went the toads outside.

Boing! Just like that, Judy had an idea. A perfect predicts-the-future idea.

She, Judy Moody, predicted Stink would give the mood ring back in no time. All she needed was a yogurt container, a little luck, and a toad.

Judy held out her umbrella and bent over, searching for toads. She looked in a pile of logs. She looked inside a loop of garden hose. She looked under the old bathtub behind the shed.

Ra-reek! Ra-reek!

She could hear about a thousand toads, but couldn't see a single one. There had to be a Toady-looking toad around here somewhere. It's not like she was looking for a rare northeast beach tiger beetle or anything.

Judy was just about to give up and go back inside when she heard something. Something close. Something right there on the back porch. Something like *Ra-reek! Ra-reek!*

It was Mouse! Mouse sounded like a toad!

The cat was drinking from her water dish.

Wait! Mouse did not sound like a toad. Mouse's water dish sounded like a toad. A real live toad was swimming in Mouse's water dish!

Judy took a deep breath. Slowly, slowly, she held out the yogurt container.

"Ha!" Judy trapped the toad under the yogurt container. She wondered if it looked like Toady. She lifted up the container to study the toad.

RA-REEK! Boing!

The toad hopped across the porch, down the steps, and into the wet grass.

"Here, Toady, Toady. Nice toad. Pretty boy. Come to Judy."

Ra-reek! Ra-reek! "Gotcha!" This time Judy caught him with her hands.

He was the same size as Toady. He had speckles and warts and bumps like Toady. He even had a white stripe down his back. Just like Toady.

"Same-same!" said Judy.

All of a sudden, Judy felt something warm and wet on her hand.

"Toady Two!" she cried.

❧   ❧   ❧

Sneaky Judy hid Toady Two under a bucket in the tent. Then she went to find Stink.

"Hey, Stink," yelled Judy, dripping in the doorway. "Let's go hunt for stuff in the backyard." Stink did not even look up from reading the *S* encyclopedia.

"*S* is for *Saturday*," said Judy. "*S* is for *Stand Up! S* is for I'm going to *Scream* if you don't come outside."

Stink flipped a page.

"Are you coming, or are you just going to sit there?" she asked.

"Sit there," said Stink.

Judy tapped her feet. She tap-tap-tapped her fingers.

"*S* is for *Shh!*" said Stink. "I'm reading about a lizard with a tail that turns blue. A skink."

"Skinks stink," said Judy. Stink ignored her.

She, Judy Moody, liked those blue-tailed skinks as much as the next person. But she was not in an *S*-is-for-*Sitting-Still* mood. She had to get Stink outside. Fast!

"I've seen a stinky skink before."

"Where?" asked Stink.

"The backyard. C'mon, Stinker. We can look for skinks!" said Judy.

"You think?" asked Stink. He closed the encyclopedia.

"Rain is perfect skink-hunting weather!" said Judy.

Stink looked for skinks in the cracks on the back porch. He looked in the flowerpot. He looked under Mouse's dish.

"What makes you think we can find a skink anyway?" asked Stink.

"ESP. Extra-special Skink Powers. Keep looking."

"I'm looking, I'm looking."

"Whoever finds a skink first gets an ice cream at Screamin' Mimi's. Wait. What's that?"

Judy closed her eyes. "Humm, baba,

humm. Nee nee nee nee nee. Ohmmmm. I feel a presence."

"A skink?"

"I hear . . . a sound."

"Is it a skink or something?" asked Stink.

"Or something," said Judy. She closed her eyes again. She pressed her fingers to her forehead. "Yes! I'm getting a color. Greenish brown."

"Everything in the backyard is greenish brown."

"I see bumps. It's bumpy," said Judy.

"Skinks are not bumpy," said Stink.

"Definitely bumpy," said Judy.

"Is it bumpy like dead leaves? Skinks love dead leaves," said Stink.

"Bumpy like warts," said Judy. "Now I see something to do with water."

Stink looked around. "It's raining. Water is everywhere."

"I said something *to do* with water," said Judy. *Bucket. Bucket.* She tried hard to send Stink an ESP, but he wasn't getting the message.

"Wait! The presence is saying something," said Judy. "Yes. It's speaking to me. Ra-reek! Ra-reek!"

"A toad?" asked Stink. "Is the presence a toad?"

"Yes," said Judy. "No. Wait. Yes!"

"A toad? For real? Toady?" asked Stink. "Is it Toady calling?"

"YES!" said Judy. "It's Toady. Toady is calling to me. RARE!"

"Where? Where is he?" asked Stink.

"Wait. No. Sorry. I had it. But I'm losing it now."

"NO!" cried Stink. "Close your eyes again. Concentrate. Feel the presence or something."

"Do it with me," said Judy. Stink and Judy held hands. They closed their eyes. "Say *eeny meany green zucchini,*" said Judy.

"Eeny greeny mean zucchini."

"Yes! I see it! I see a bucket. And I see something blue. A blue roof? No. It's a tent. Yes. A blue tent!"

Stink raced inside the tent and went straight for the bucket. He lifted it up.

Ra-reek!

"Toady Two!" said Judy.

"Toady Two?"

"I mean Toady, t-o-o. As in *also*. As in not just some crummy old bucket."

"Toady! You're back!" cried Stink. He hugged the toad in his hands. He grinned a loose-tooth grin. "I missed you. You came back. For real. Just like Judy said."

"Like I predicted," said Judy. "Just call me Madame Moody. Madame M for short."

"Is it really him?" said Stink.

"Who else?"

"Toady, I didn't let you go. Judy did. Honest. Don't ever leave again."

Stink held Toady in both hands. "I don't even care if he makes me a member of the

Toad Pee Club again," said Stink.

"Ick," said Judy.

Stink kissed Toady on his beady-eyed, bumpy little head.

"Now can I have my ring back?" she asked.

Madame M for Moody

Judy and Stink came in out of the rain. They ate Fig Newtons and sipped hot chocolate with fancy straws.

"You really are psychic," said Stink.

"Told you," said Judy. She chomped on her cookie.

"I thought it was just another one of your tricks," said Stink.

"Uh-huh." *Chomp, chomp.*

"Toady came back. And you knew. You predicted it."

"Uh-huh."

"At first I didn't believe you," said Stink. "But then I saw the little black stripe."

Judy's Fig almost fell out of her Newton. "What little black stripe?"

"The little black stripe over Toady's right eye. No other toads have it. Just Toady. That's how I knew it was him."

"Let me see that toad," said Judy.

Stink took Toady out of the yogurt container. Dr. Judy Moody examined the toad like she was giving a checkup. Stink was right. He did have a little black stripe, just like Toady. Could it be?

She, Judy Moody, predicted that Toady came back, and . . . he did?

"You can have your mood ring back," said Stink.

"Huh?"

"Your mood ring?" said Stink. "You were right. It really does belong to a person with superduper special powers. Here. Take it." Stink wiggled the ring, but it was stuck.

"*S* is for *Stuck*!" said Stink. He held out his hand. "I can't get it off! Ack!! My finger! It's green!"

"Stink, it's okay."

"But you predicted my finger would turn green and fall off. Look! Now it *is* green! Hurry up. Before my finger falls off."

"*S* is for *Soap,*" said Judy.

Judy took Stink over to the sink and soaped up his finger. She twirled the ring. She twisted the ring. She pulled the ring. She yanked the ring. *POP!*

"Mine at last," said Madame *M*-for-*Moody* Judy.

☙   ☙   ☙

On Monday morning, Judy Moody woke up early. What might have been a blucky old math-test Monday did not seem blucky one bit.

She did not put on her tiger-striped pajamas for school. She did not put on her I ATE A SHARK T-shirt. She put on her best-mood-ever clothes — purple striped pants, a not-itchy fuzzy green sweater with a star, and Screamin' Mimi's ice-cream-cone socks. And her mood ring.

Light blue! Light blue was the next best thing to purple. Light blue meant *Happy, Glad.* She was glad to have her ring back. She was happy with the world.

"Purr-fect!" she said to Mouse. Mouse rubbed up against her leg.

On the bus, she told good-mood jokes. "Why did the third grader eat so many corn flakes?" Judy asked her friend Rocky.

"I don't know. Because all the snowflakes were melted?" asked Rocky.

"No!" said Judy. "To get a mood ring!" Judy cracked herself up.

She told jokes all the way to school. Stink plugged his ears. Rocky just shuffled his deck of magic cards.

"You're not laughing at my jokes," Judy complained.

"Um, I'm worried about Mr. Todd's math test," said Rocky. "Fractions!"

Normally Judy would have worried too. Not today. Her mood ring had just turned blue-green for *Relaxed, Calm.*

☺   ☺   ☺

"Okay, class," said Mr. Todd. "A new week. I know we have a few tests this week. Math test today. Spelling test on Wednesday. But don't forget, we have a special visitor next week. Monday. One week from today. A real live author! She's also an artist. She wrote and illustrated a book about crayons."

"A baby book?" asked Rocky.

"I think you'll find it interesting," said Mr. Todd. "There's so much to know about crayons." Mr. Todd grinned. Since when did crayons make her teacher so happy?

In Reading, Mr. Todd read *The Case of the Red-Eyed Mummy*. Judy solved it before anyone else did.

When it came time to write a mystery in her journal, Judy wrote *The Mystery of the Missing Mood Ring,* in which she, Judy Moody, solved the case.

All morning, Judy raised her mood-ring hand, even when she didn't know the answer.

Even Mr. Todd noticed the ring. "What's that you've got there?" he asked Judy.

"A mood ring," Judy said. "It predicts stuff. Like what mood you're in."

"Very nice," said Mr. Todd.

"Let's hope everybody's in the mood for the math test. Class 3T, put all books away, please."

Judy leaned over and asked her friend Frank Pearl if he had studied his fractions.

"Yep," said Frank. "But I'll be half happy and half glad when it's over."

Judy looked over her shoulder at Jessica Finch. She looked *Relaxed, Calm.* Jessica Finch probably ate fractions for breakfast: 1/4 glass of orange juice, 1/2 piece of toast, 3/4 jar of strawberry jelly!

Judy took her time on the test. She did not bite off her Grouchy pencil eraser. She did not make grouchy faces at the math test. She was even *Relaxed, Calm* about making up a word problem.

Problem

A rainbow has seven colors (ROY G. BIV)
If Judy has a purple mood ring, Rocky
has a blue mood ring, Frank has a
red mood ring, and Stink has a green
mood ring, how much of the rainbow
do they have? (Answer has to be a
fraction!)

Hint: There are four mood rings, or four
out of seven colors of the rainbow.

ANSWER: 4/7!

At recess, everybody crowded around Judy. "Where'd you get that mood ring?"

"Ooh, let me try!"

Time to daze and amaze her friends.

"Who wants to go first?" asked Judy.

"Me me me me me!" Everybody pushed and shoved and begged.

"Wait," said Judy. "Before anyone puts the ring on, I'm going to make a prediction."

Judy looked at the chart that came with the mood ring. Amber meant *Nervous, Tense.* Rocky was nervous about the math test.

"Madame M predicts the ring will turn amber on Rocky," said Judy. Rocky slid the ring onto his finger. It turned black.

"Madame M is W-R-O-N-G!" said Rocky.

"Just wait!" Judy said. "The mood ring doesn't lie." Everybody crowded around Rocky to watch. Slowly, it did turn amber, just like Judy said!

"How did you know?" asked Rocky.

"Madame M knows all," said Judy. "I predict it will be light blue on Frank. I can feel it," said Judy.

"Is blue sad?" asked Frank. "Because I don't feel sad. And I don't want to think of sad things. Like the time I didn't have a club for my Me Collage and the time I was a human centipede and somebody broke my finger."

"Boo-hoo. *Dark* blue is *Unhappy, Sad.* C'mon, just try the ring on!"

Frank slipped the ring onto his finger.

Judy crossed her fingers and whispered to herself, "Light blue, light blue, light blue." Not a minute later the ring turned light blue.

"Same-same!" said Judy. "Light blue is *Happy, Glad.* That's the color it turned on me, too."

"Ooh-ooh! Frank got the same color as Judy!"

"Frank Pearl and Judy are in love!" everybody teased.

"Frank Pearl's getting married. To Judy Moody! And he already has the ring!" Frank turned bright red. He practically threw the ring at Jessica Finch.

"I hope it's pink on me," said Jessica.

"There is no pink," said Judy. "But there's GREEN," she said loudly to the ring.

Before Jessica could try the ring on, the bell rang and recess was over.

☙   ☙   ☙

In Science, Mr. Todd was talking about weather and the world's temperature rising. Judy sharpened her pencil with her mood-ring hand. She threw trash in the trash can with her mood-ring hand. She passed a note to Frank with her mood-ring hand.

Judy did not see Mr. Todd's temperature rising!

"I wish I had a mood ring," whispered Jessica Finch.

"You have to eat a lot of cereal," Judy whispered back, a little too loudly.

"Judy, is there a problem?" asked Mr. Todd.

"No," said Judy, sitting on her hands.

As soon as Mr. Todd turned back to the board, Judy played with her ring to make Jessica jealous. She twisted the ring. She twirled the ring. She spun the ring on her finger. It flew off, hit Mr. Todd's desk, and landed at Mr. Todd's feet.

Mr. Todd bent over and picked it up. "Judy," he said, "I'm afraid I'll have to keep the ring for you until the end of the day."

Judy turned one, two, three shades of red. Even Madame M had not predicted the mood ring would get her into trouble.

Mr. Todd slipped the ring onto the top of his index finger. He opened his desk drawer. As he put it away, Judy thought she caught a glimpse of color.

Could it be? No. Wait. Maybe. It was! YES! Judy was 3/4 sure. She was 9/10 sure. Mr. Todd might have the ring, but she, Judy Moody, had seen red. Red as in Red Hots. Red as in ruby slippers.

RARE squared!

The Sleeping Speller

That night, Judy met Frank at the library to study for the spelling test.

"Hey! You got your mood ring back from Mr. Todd," said Frank when Judy arrived.

"Yes!" said Judy, holding up her hand to admire it. She would never, ever, not ever take her mood ring off again until it turned positively purple. Except at school, of course. Mr. Todd said no more mood rings at school. While she was at school, she would be sure to keep it safe. Hidden in her extra-special baby-tooth box.

"Speaking of Mr. Todd, have you seen the spelling words?" asked Frank. "They are hard, as in D-I-F-F-I-C-U-L-T!"

Judy looked at the list. "*Woodbine!* What in the world's a woodbine?"

"Who knows?" asked Frank.

Frank went to get the big dictionary. He came back carrying it like it weighed a hundred pounds. They opened it on the table.

"'*Wood-bine,*' Judy read out loud. "'A vine that wraps around trees.'"

"'Also called Virginia creeper,'" read Frank.

"RARE!" said Judy.

"Creepy!" said Frank.

"I'm tired of studying," said Judy.

"Tired?! We only learned one word!" said Frank.

"Let's look at books," said Judy.

Frank followed Judy down a long row of high shelves. "Ooh. What books are these? It's all dark and dusty."

"I hope there aren't any Virginia-creepy vines around here," said Judy in a spooky voice.

Frank found a book with pictures of bones and the creepy insides of stuff. "Body parts!" he said.

Judy went to find the librarian.

"What did you get?" Frank asked when she came back.

"Predict Your Head Off!" said Judy. "It's all about people who predicted stuff about the future. Lynn helped me find it. She's the cool librarian with the fork-and-pie earrings. Not the mad-face librarian."

"Hey! It's a Big Head book. I love those. How come they draw the people with such big heads, anyway?" Frank asked.

"Maybe it's to hold all those big ideas about the future. Look, see?" said Judy, pointing to her book. "These people predicted earthquakes and fires and babies being born."

"Nobody can predict the future," said Frank. "Can they?"

"Ya-huh!" said Judy. "It says right here. Books don't lie."

"Let me see," said Frank.

"See? Jeane Dixon, Famous American Fortuneteller. She was some lady in Washington, D.C., who stared into her eggs one morning and predicted that President Kennedy would be shot. And she predicted an earthquake in Alaska."

"It also says she predicted that Martians would come to Earth and take away teenagers. I wish that would happen to my big sister."

"If only Stink were a teenager," said Judy.

"Look! It says here that that Jeane Dixon lady saw stuff in whipped cream!" said Frank.

"I've seen stuff in whipped cream, too," said Judy. "Lots of times."

"Like what?"

"Like chocolate sprinkles," Judy said, and they both cracked up.

"Hey, look at this," said Judy. "This book can help us with our spelling test. For real."

"No way."

"Way! See this guy?"

"The bald guy with the bow tie?"

"Yep. It says that he lived right here in Virginia. They called him the Sleeping Prophet. When he was our age, like a hundred years ago, he got into trouble in school for being a bad speller. One night he fell asleep with his spelling book under his head. When he woke up, he knew every word in the book. RARE!"

"I'm still going to study," said Frank.

"Not me!" said Judy, wiggling into her coat.

"What are you going to do?" asked Frank.

"I'm going to go home and sleep," said Judy.

❧   ❧   ❧

When Judy got home, Stink was at the door.

"I don't have to study for my spelling test," she said, and gave him a big fat hug.

"What's that for?" asked Stink.

"That's for just because."

"Just because why?"

"Just because tomorrow I am going to know tons and tons of words, like *woodbine*."

"Wood what?"

"It's a creepy vine. It wraps around trees."

"So go find a tree to hug," said Stink.

Instead, Judy went to find the dictionary. The fattest dictionary in the Moody house. She took it from her mom's office and lugged it up to her room. She did not open it up. She did not look inside. She put the big red dictionary under her pillow. Then she got into her cozy bowling-ball

pajamas. She pretended the bowling balls were crystal balls. When she brushed her teeth, she thought she saw a letter in her toothpaste spit. *D* for *Dictionary*.

Judy climbed under the covers and leaned back on her pillow. Youch! Too hard. She got two more pillows. At last, she was ready to dream.

Even before she fell asleep, she dreamed of being Queen of the Spelling Bee, just like Jessica Finch was one time for the whole state of Virginia. She dreamed of Mr. Todd's smiling face when he passed back the tests. Most of all, she dreamed of getting 110% — zero-wrong-plus-extra-credit — on her spelling test.

She could hardly wait for school tomorrow. For once, she, Judy Moody, not Jessica (Flunk) Finch, would get a Thomas Jefferson tricorn-hat sticker for *Great Job, Good Thinking.*

ZZZZZZZZZzzzzzzzz...

Preposterous Hippopotamus

When Judy woke up the next morning, her neck was so stiff she felt like a crookneck squash. But her head did not feel the least bit bigger. It did not even feel heavy from carrying around so many new words. She looked in the mirror. Same Judy-head as always.

At breakfast, Judy stared into her eggs, just like Jeane Dixon, Famous American

Fortuneteller. She thought she felt an earthquake! The earthquake was Stink, shaking the ketchup bottle onto his eggs.

"Stink, that's *preposterous*!" said Judy.

"What's that mean?" asked Stink.

"It means *ridiculous*," said Judy.

"Like funny or silly," said Mom.

"Think *hippopotamus*," said Judy.

RARE! The dictionary-under-the-pillow thing really worked! Big words were flying out of her mouth faster than spit.

Judy was in a positively purple, On-Top-of-Spaghetti-and-the-World mood. She wished she could take her mood ring to school. If only.

On the bus, Judy told Rocky that his new magic trick was *bewildering*.

At school, Frank gave Judy a miniature hotel soap from his collection. "I already have this one," he said. Judy told him his treat was very *unexpected*.

Then she asked Jessica (Flunk) Finch if she looked forward to the spelling test with *anticipation*.

"Why are you talking funny?" asked Jessica.

Mr. Todd passed out lined paper for the test. He told the class, "Only three more school days until our special visitor comes to class."

Something was not the same. Something was different. Something was *peculiar, unusual.* Mr. Todd had new glasses! And he was wearing a tie. A crayon tie! Mr. Todd had never dressed up for a spelling test before.

"Your new glasses are very *noticeable,*" said Judy.

"Thank you, Judy," said Mr. Todd with a goofy grin.

During the test, Judy Moody's Grouchy pencil flew across the page like never before. She spelled *alfalfa* and *applesauce.* She spelled *cobweb* and *crystal.* She hardly even had to erase, except on *zucchini.*

And she used the extra-credit word in a sentence! *Crayon.* What kind of a bonus word was *crayon*? Mr. Todd had crayons on the brain. For sure and absolute positive.

Madame M predicts that the Crayon Lady will soon come to Class 3T to see Mr. Todd's crayon tie.

Judy's extra-credit word sentence was practically a paragraph! And she used the bonus word twice! Double R-A-R-E!

Judy was the first one to finish, even before the Queen Bee Speller Jessica Finch. Jessica wasn't even using her lucky pencil! What was that girl thinking?

At the lunch table, she, Judy Moody, was in a predict-the-future mood.

"Don't open your lunches yet," Judy

said to everybody. "Madame M will predict what's inside."

"Hurry up," said Rocky. "I'm hungry."

Judy shut her eyes. This was so easy. "I see baloney. Baloney sandwiches." Rocky, Frank, and Jessica each held up a baloney sandwich.

Everyone was amazed.

Now the moment she'd been waiting for. "I have another prediction," said Judy in a loud voice. "One about tomorrow. Something big. Something that's never happened in Class 3T before."

"Really? Tell us! What?"

"I, Judy Moody, will get zero-wrong-plus-extra-credit on the spelling test! 110%! Pass it on."

"That's as preposterous as a H-I-P-P-O-P-O-T-A-M-U-S," Jessica said.

"You didn't even study," Frank said.

"You never even got 100% in Spelling," said Rocky.

"Thanks a lot," said Judy. What a bunch of baloney eaters. "That was before I became the Sleeping Speller, before I learned about sleeping with the dictionary under my pillow."

"But Mr. Todd didn't pass our tests back yet," said Frank. "You don't even know if it really worked."

Judy rolled her eyeballs around. She made thinking noises. "Humm, baba, humm. Mr. Todd is correcting the papers right now. I see a Thomas Jefferson sticker.

A tricorn hat. For *Great Job, Good Thinking*."

"You're 110% cuckoo," Rocky told Judy.

"Just call me the Sleeping Speller," Judy said.

Antarctica

Judy predicted it would be hard to sit still until Mr. Todd passed back the spelling tests. She predicted right. She felt antsy as an anthill. Jumpy as a jumping bean.

At last, the time came.

"Good work. Keep it up," Mr. Todd was saying as he walked around the room, passing back tests and handing out cookies. Heart-shaped cookies. With sprinkles!

And he was humming. Mr. Todd never hummed! And he never brought heart-shaped cookies with sprinkles. Not even on Valentine's Day, which it wasn't.

It had to be a sign. A sign that she, the Sleeping Speller, had done superduper *stupendous* on her spelling test. That would definitely put Mr. Todd in a good mood.

In less than one minute, Class 3T would see that she, Madame M, had ESP. Extra-special Spelling Powers. Just like Jeane Dixon, Famous American Fortuneteller. And Sleeping Speller Man.

In less than one minute, Judy had her test back. And the only cookie left was a broken heart.

Dear Mr. President! Something was not right! Her paper did not have a Thomas Jefferson sticker. It did not even have a president. Or a sticker. It had a feather. A musty, dusty-looking, old-timey rubber-stamp feather. A quill pen. A quill pen meant *Keep Trying*. A quill pen meant *You Have More Work to Do*. A quill pen was as *preposterous* as a *hippopotamus*.

At the bottom of her test was a note from Mr. Todd. It said, "*Tortilla* has two *l*'s. *Zigzag* is one word."

Judy didn't see why *tor-tee-yah* had any *l*'s at all. And *zig* and *zag* sure seemed like two words to her. Who wrote the dictionary anyway? Mrs. Merriam and Mr. Webster were going to hear from her.

All eyes were on Judy. She turned fire-engine red. Hide-your-face-in your-hands red. Big-fat-dictionary red.

The Sleeping Speller was a flop. The Sleeping Speller was a flubber-upper. The Sleeping Speller was a big fat phoney-baloney.

Maybe Jessica (Flunk) Finch got a musty, dusty quill pen, too! Judy knew it was a bad-mood thought. Judy knew she was supposed to keep her eyes on her own paper. But she couldn't help herself. She turned around.

Jessica Finch beamed. Jessica Finch gleamed. Like the day she was crowned Queen Bee and got her picture in the paper. Jessica Finch sat up straight and

proud as a president. She held up her paper
for Judy to see.

"I knew it!" Jessica said. "I got a Thomas
Jefferson tricorn hat!"

A tricorn hat did not mean *flubber-upper.*
A tricorn hat did not mean *Better luck next
time. Keep trying. You need more practice!* A
tricorn hat meant *Hats off to you!*

"How did you know?" Judy asked. Judy was supposed to be the one predicting the future, not Jessica Finch.

"I used my brain," said Jessica. "Some people studied."

Judy was green with *Jealous, Envy*. And she did not need her mood ring to prove it.

The class buzzed. They turned on Judy like a pack of stinging bees.

"Hey, what happened to the Sleeping Speller?"

"The Sleeping Speller fell asleep!"

Judy Moody gave them all a Virginia creeper stare.

"Hold on, everybody," said Mr. Todd-the-Hummer. "You know that in this class we keep our eyes on our own papers."

"But Mr. Todd, Judy Moody *said*. She told us. She predicted she would get a 110% perfect paper. She predicted WRONG!"

"Nobody can really predict the future!" said Rocky. "Right, Mr. Todd?"

"Well, we all play a part in creating our own futures," said Mr. Todd. "So, in the future, I hope you'll concern yourselves with your own work, not the work of the person next to you."

That got everybody quiet.

"Now. Let's move on to . . . science. Take out your Weather Notebooks."

Judy did not take out her Weather Notebook. She was comparing her paper to Jessica Finch's.

"Judy," said Mr. Todd, "I'm afraid you haven't heard a word I've said. I'm going to have to ask you to go to Antarctica."

Antarctica!

Antarctica was a desk in the back of the room with a map on top. A map with a lot of icebergs and a lot of penguins. And a sign that said CHILL OUT. The sign might as well have said IN BIG TROUBLE.

Judy looked at Mr. Todd. He did not look one bit like the Hummer, Mr. New Glasses, Mr. Crayon Tie, the teacher who brought heart-shaped cookies to class. He looked like Mr. Toad.

Judy hung her head and walked to the desk in the back of the room. Jessica Finch

was Thomas Jefferson. And she, Judy Moody, was president of Antarctica.

Judy was mad enough to spit. How could Madame M ever predict the future if she could not even predict one lousy spelling test?

One thing she could predict was the weather. It was cold in Antarctica. Cold enough to freeze spit.

"Okay," said Mr. Todd. "Time for the weather reports. Who wants to be our meteorologist for the day? Any predictions?"

Weather report from Antarctica: Cloudy with a chance of never getting a Thomas Jefferson sticker.

The V.I.Q.

On the way back to her seat, Jessica Finch asked Judy, "How was Antarctica?"

"Long," said Judy.

What did Jessica Finch care anyway? She probably knew how to spell *Antarctica*. Even without sleeping on the dictionary.

Judy grumped. Judy slumped. Judy Moody was down in the dumps. The dumpiest. She, Madame M for Mistake, could not predict the future — her own or anybody else's. She could not even predict one hour from now. Not one minute. Not one second. The future was *un-predictable.*

That did it. Judy decided then and there she would give up predicting the future. For-ever. She had the Moody blues, the Judy-Moodiest.

She dragged herself to the water fountain at afternoon recess.

"Hel-lo? Judy? What is wrong with you?" asked Jessica Finch.

"I'm a flop. A big fat fake. I can't tell the future. Just call me Madame Phoney-Baloney."

"Okay, Madame Phoney-Baloney!" said Jessica Finch. She laughed like a hyena. "If you say so. But I know something that tells the future. You can ask a question and it's N-E-V-E-R wrong."

Judy sprayed herself with water. How did Jessica Finch know so much about future-telling? "Really?"

"Really."

"Never?"

"Never!" said Jessica. "I'll bring it tomorrow. Think of something you want to ask. Something on your mind. Something that's been bugging you — a V.I.Q."

"V.I.Q.?"

"Very Important Question," said Jessica.

⟖   ⟖   ⟖

Judy could hardly wait. She could hardly think about anything else. She could hardly sleep, even without the fat red dictionary under her pillow.

Judy thought and thought. She thought about something that had been on her mind. She thought about something that had been bugging her. She came up with a very important V.I.Q.

Judy got to school early Thursday morning. She rushed up to Jessica Finch. "Did you bring it? Did you?"

Jessica opened her pink plastic backpack and took out a bright yellow ball with a big smiley face on the outside. "Magic 8 Ball!" said Jessica.

"That's not a Magic 8 Ball," said Judy.

"Is too," said Jessica. "I'll show you."

"Will I always be the best speller at Virginia Dare School?" Jessica asked the Magic 8 Ball. The answer appeared in the window on a little triangle floating in blue liquid.

You're a winner.

"See? You try," said Jessica.

Judy decided to ask a practice question first. "Will my mood ring ever turn purple?" Judy shook the ball.

You look marvelous.

"Try again," said Jessica.

"Will my mood ring ever turn purple?"

Nice outfit.

"You're not asking right," said Jessica.

Judy shook the ball extra hard. "Will I be a doctor someday?"

Pure genius.

"Will I ever get a 110% Thomas Jefferson sticker on my spelling test?

You're 100% fun.

"Will Mom and Dad be mad about my spelling test?"

Your breath is so minty!

"These aren't answers," said Judy. "Why is it saying all goopy stuff?"

"It's the Happy 8 Ball," said Jessica. "It only gives you good answers."

"No fair!" said Judy. "The Happy 8 Ball is a fake!"

"A good fake," said Jessica.

"I'm not going to ask my V.I.Q. I'll get a good answer, no matter what."

"Exactly," said Jessica.

"How can you believe what the Happy 8 Ball predicts if it just says goopy, good stuff all the time?" asked Judy.

"I don't care," said Jessica. "I like the Happy 8 Ball."

"I need an Un-happy 8 Ball!" said Judy.

"The one that doesn't lie."

And she knew just where to get it.

                                     @   @   @

Judy talked Rocky and Frank into going with her to Vic's Mini-Mart after school. Stink came too.

"I hope you're not getting a fake hand to play another trick on me," said Stink.

"No," said Judy. "I'm getting a crystal ball."

When they got to Vic's, Judy led them all to the toy section. They saw troll doll trading cards, an eyeball piggy bank, and

some cat erasers. Then Judy spied one. A black ball with the real number 8 on it in a white circle.

"Magic 8 Ball!" said Judy. "The real one."

"That crystal ball is plastic," said Stink.

"It still tells the future," said Judy.

She held the Magic 8 Ball in the palm of her hand. She could almost feel its magic predicting powers.

"We can each ask one question," said Judy. "Who dares to ask the All-Knowing Magic 8 Ball first?

"Me, me, me!" said Frank.

"Okay," said Judy, handing him the ball.

"Will I get a Jawbreaker Maker for my birthday?" asked Frank.

"You forgot to close your eyes tight and concentrate," said Judy.

Frank closed his eyes tight. Frank concentrated. He asked again. He shook the Magic 8 Ball. They all leaned over and peered into the tiny window.

Outlook not so good.

"I hope this thing lies," said Frank.

"Me next," said Rocky, taking the 8 Ball and shaking it. "Does Frank Pearl love Judy Moody?"

Signs point to yes.

"That's so funny I forgot to laugh," said Frank.

"Give me that," said Judy.

"My turn," said Stink.

"You only get one question, so think hard," Judy said. "And hurry up."

"Am I going to be president someday?" asked Stink.

Don't count on it.

"Will my little brother ever stop driving me crazy?" asked Judy.

Better not tell you now.

Stink grabbed the Magic 8 Ball back. "Does Rocky love Judy?"

"Do not anger the Magic 8 Ball," said the spooky-voiced Madame M. She peered into the little window. "Air bubble! See? You used up all your questions," Madame M pronounced. "We have to put it back now."

"How come?"

"Air bubble! It's the rules!"

Stink, Rocky, and Frank went to buy gumballs.

"I'll catch up," Judy called.

Judy Moody did not put the Magic 8 Ball back on the shelf. She had one final question. The thing that had been bugging her for days. The V.I.Q.

Judy looked around. She concentrated. She shook the Magic 8 Ball. "Is Mr. Todd in love?" Judy whispered.

Reply hazy, try again.

Judy closed her eyes. She held her breath. She said some magic words. "Eeny meany jelly beany," said Judy. "Is Mr. Todd in love?"

She shook the Magic 8 Ball. She shook it

some more. At last, she opened her eyes.

There it was. The answer. In the window. A small triangle floating in blue liquid.

Yes, definitely.

Operation True Love

Judy stretched out on her top bunk and stared up at the glow-in-the-dark stars on her ceiling. It all added up. The red ring. The new glasses, the humming, the heart-shaped cookies. It was right there all the time. Her best-ever prediction. All she had to do was see it. Use her brain. Make the connection. Mr. Todd was in love!

At last, she, Madame M, could predict

something really, truly big. Something really, truly true. Something only she, Judy Moody, knew about. Judy had a new plan. A perfect, foolproof, fail-safe, predicts-the-future plan. All she had to do now was trick Mr. Todd into trying on the mood ring. She had to see once and for all if it turned red for *Romantic, In Love.*

Only one thing stood in the way. She was not allowed to bring the mood ring to school.

On Friday morning, Judy took out her mood ring. She did not wear it on her finger. She did not show it to anyone. She kept it hidden in her baby-tooth box. She kept that hidden in the secret pocket of her backpack. Until after school.

Time for Project Mood Ring. Operation True Love. She, Dr. Judy Moody, was 3/4 sure and 9/10 certain that the Magic 8 Ball did not lie. But she had to be 110% sure-and-absolute positive.

"Mr. Todd," said Judy, taking her mood ring out of the secret box. "I know I'm not supposed to bring my mood ring to school and everything, but I have a V.I.Q. A Very Important Question."

"I'm going to be in a bad mood if I see that ring in class again."

"I kept it put away all day," said Judy. "I promise. I was just hoping I could ask you how a mood ring works. In the name of science and everything."

"Mood rings *are* interesting," said Mr. Todd. "They used to be popular when I was a kid, you know."

"No way!" said Judy.

"Way!" said Mr. Todd, laughing. "Here, let me see that ring again."

Mr. Todd held the ring with his fingers.

Judy tried to ESP Mr. Todd a message. *Put the ring on. Put the ring on.*

"Mood rings have their own science."

Put the ring on.

"Did you know our bodies give off heat energy?"

Put the ring on.

Mr. Todd slipped the ring onto his index finger. "Liquid crystals change color as our bodies change temperature. See? Red is for hot."

It worked! Red! The ring was r-e-d, red. Red for *Romantic.* Red for *In Love.* Red for sure and absolute positive.

"It is hot in here, isn't it?" said Mr. Todd.

"*Red* hot," said Judy. "Hot enough to melt Antarctica."

"I'm afraid Antarctica is here to stay," said Mr. Todd. He handed her the ring. "Does that answer your Very Important Question?"

"Yes, yes, yes!" said Judy. "Thanks, Mr. Todd!" Judy dashed out the door.

Madame M was back in business. And she was going to predict a future better than ever. Judy kissed her mood ring!

As soon as she reached the bus, she slipped it onto her finger. The ring turned amber. Amber meant *Nervous, Tense*. She knew what she was nervous about: her Judy Moody best-ever prediction. Before she could tell anybody, she had to figure out *who* Mr. Todd was in love with. That was not going to be easy.

❧   ❧   ❧

On Saturday morning, Judy went back to the library. She looked for Lynn, the friendly librarian with the fork-and-pie earrings.

Today, Lynn had skateboard earrings.

"You changed your earrings!" said Judy.

"I do that sometimes," said Lynn, and she laughed. "What can I help you with?"

"Where are the books that tell you if a person is in love?"

"Well, you know," Lynn said, "that kind of thing is hard to find in a book. Usually a person just sort of knows. Inside."

"Just so you know, it's not for me," Judy said, turning three shades of red. "I'm trying to figure out if someone else is in love."

"Ah. I see."

"You have a million gazillion books. There must be something in here with lovey-dovey stuff. Everybody likes love."

"Let me think a minute," said Lynn. "We do have Valentine's Day books. And love stories."

"No magic charms? Secret spells?"

"Let's try the 100's," Lynn said. She led Judy right to the love section and pulled a purple book with silver writing off the shelf. The silver writing said, *Find Your True Love.* Judy opened it up and flipped through the pages. Chapter Five was titled, "All You Need Is a Bowl of Molasses!"

"Molasses! That's easy! I'll take it!" said Judy. "Thanks!"

Judy read the book while she waited in line to check out. She read it as she walked home. She read it walking into her house.

In ancient times, staring into a bowl of molasses might reveal the identity of a true love.

Judy went straight to the kitchen and poured a jar of thick, sticky molasses into a bowl. She added some magic words. "Eeny meany chili beany. Who does Mr. Todd love?" She stared and stared into the molasses.

What she saw looked a little like . . . a chicken.

No way! Mr. Todd was not in love with a chicken.

Instead of molasses, people in Egypt looked into pools of ink.

Judy got a bottle of rubber-stamp ink from the desk in the hall. When she poured it into a bowl, all she saw was a big fat mess. And an ink splat on her shirt that looked like Antarctica. Nobody was in love with Antarctica.

Place a dish on a table and drop twenty-one safety pins into it.

She skipped that one. She did not have twenty-one pins, safe or unsafe.

Place a piece of wedding cake under your pillow and dream of the person you'll marry.

Wedding cake! Where on earth was she supposed to find wedding cake?

You will need a clock and a hairbrush.

Hairbrush! Judy had never met a hair-brush she liked. What did a hairbrush have to do with true love anyway? This love stuff sure was complicated!

Cut out twenty-six squares of paper, one for each letter of the alphabet. Place the letters of the alphabet face down in a bowl of water. The letters that turn face up will spell a loved one's name.

Bowl of water. Letters. She circled it. She could trick Mr. Todd into that!

Press an apple seed to the forehead and recite the letters of the alphabet. When the seed falls off, that's the letter of the true love's name.

Apple seed. She could do that, too! She drew stars around that one.

Light a candle. If the wax drips to the left side, a woman is in love. Right side, a man is in love.

RARE!

Judy wrote a note to herself:

Bowl of water + Apple Seed + Candle = true Love

Non-Fiction Prediction

Judy was first to arrive in Room 3T on Monday morning.

"Judy, would you pass out crayons to everybody?" asked Mr. Todd.

"What for?"

"Today we're going to do all our writing with crayons."

"What for?" Judy asked.

"For fun!"

"Magic Markers are better," said Judy. Mr. Todd frowned.

"I'm just saying."

"But don't you just love the smell of crayons?" asked Mr. Todd.

Judy hurried up and passed out the not-Magic-Marker crayons. Then she asked Mr. Crayon Smeller if she could conduct a scientific experiment on his desk.

She set a bowl of water with twenty-six paper letters next to his pencil jar.

She could hardly wait to see which letters turned right side up. Soon she, Madame M, would know the name of Mr. Todd's secret love! She would no longer be Madame M for Mistake. No more Phoney-Baloney.

During Science class, Judy watched the letters float upside down in the bowl of water. Mr. Todd was talking away about cumulus clouds. Judy drew puffy clouds with her Blizzard Blue crayon. She drew skinny clouds. She drew clouds shaped like hearts and crayons.

As soon as Science was over, Judy

rushed up to Mr. Todd's desk. Lots of the upside-down paper squares had turned over! But all the Magic Marker letters had gotten runny and blurry in the water. She could not read one single letter!

"Did your experiment work?" asked Mr. Todd.

"No," said Judy. "It came out a big fat zero."

"Try again," said Mr. Todd. "True science takes time."

Yes, thought Judy. But this time she would use an apple seed.

Judy ate the apple at lunch. At recess, she found Mr. Todd on the playground talking with Rocky and Frank. "Mr. Todd," Judy asked, "will you help me with another experiment?"

"Anything for science," said Mr. Todd.

"Put this apple seed on your forehead. Then say the alphabet."

"Fun-ny!" said Frank.

"Are you going to?" asked Rocky.

"Somehow this doesn't exactly sound scientific," said Mr. Todd. He stuck the apple seed to his forehead. He started singing the alphabet song. "A B C D, E F G . . ." All the kids laughed.

"Is this a joke?" asked Mr. Todd.

"Don't stop!" cried Judy. "You'll wreck the experiment!"

Mr. Todd sang all the way to the letter *T* before the apple seed fell off.

The letter T, thought Judy. *Hmm. Same as Todd.*

"How'd I do?" asked Mr. Todd.

"We'll see," said Judy. "True science takes time."

"Glad I could help. Now we'd better head back inside. Don't forget, today's the big day. Our special guest author is coming to visit 3T."

"You mean the Crayon Lady?" asked Frank. "Today?"

"How could you forget?" asked Judy. "Mr. Todd's had crayons on the brain for a whole week."

Who cared about crayons anyway? Crayons were for kindergartners. She had grown-up things to think about. Important things. Like L-O-V-E, love.

◎   ◎   ◎

Class 3T washed the blackboard and picked up scraps of paper under their chairs. They fed the fish and emptied the trash and erased pencil marks on their desks. Mr. Todd wanted the room to look extra special, extra sparkling.

"We've never had to clean this much for anybody," said Frank.

"Tell me about it," said Judy. "Who's going to look in the trash anyway?"

"Her?" said Frank, pointing to a woman tapping on their door.

As soon as she came in, Class 3T put

123

on their best third-grade listening ears.

"Class 3T," said Mr. Todd, "I would like you to meet a special friend of mine, Ms. Tater. As you know, she's an author and an artist, and she's here today all the way from New York to tell us about the book she wrote called *Crayons Aren't for Eating*."

Everybody clapped. The Crayon Lady looked like a crayon! She wore a lemon yellow top and a skirt like a painting. She had short, curly boy-hair and a fancy scarf around her head. She even had on crayon earrings. Best of all, she had melted orange crayon wax on her boots!

Ms. Tater showed 3T her book about how crayons were made. She told the class it was *non-fiction*. *Non-fiction* meant the opposite of *fiction*. It meant true.

Ms. Tater was non-old (young). She was non-ugly (pretty). And she was non-boring (interesting). She told the class how the first crayon was made a hundred years ago. She told about the secret formula for crayons, made of wax, color, and powder.

Then the author lit a candle and mixed the candle wax drips with red powder to show how they make crayons. "It's like mixing flour in a cake mix," said Ms. Tater.

Ms. Tater told them how one time she met some famous guy named Captain Kangaroo at a crayon museum in New York. No lie.

She even told about the Crayon Eater machine. It was a big machine that checked for broken or lumpy crayons and threw the bad ones out.

Once, Ms. Tater got to name her own crayon.

"What was it called?" everybody asked.

"Pumpkin Moon," she said, and she held up an orange crayon that matched her boots. "Mr. Todd helped me think of it." Her smile was Nightlight Bright.

"Some new names of crayons are Atomic Tangerine, Banana Mania, and Eggplant."

Eggplant *was* a color! Stink was right! "Is Zucchini a crayon?" asked Judy.

"No, but that's a good idea," said Ms.

Tater. "And then there's my favorite: Purple Mountain Majesty."

"RARE!" said Judy. Purple Mountain Majesty! That was as good as Joyful, On-Top-of-the-World purple.

"Mr. Todd's favorite is Vermilion."

"That's red," said Mr. Todd.

Red! Judy sat up straight as a president and perked up her best third-grade listening ears.

"And we can't forget about Macaroni and Cheese!" Ms. Tater held up a cheesy-looking crayon. "This one looks good enough to eat! But we'll leave that to the Crayon Eater machine." Everybody in Class 3T cracked up.

"Now it's your turn," Ms. Tater said.

"Who can think up a good name for a crayon? Any ideas?"

"Baseball-Mitt Brown!" said Frank.

"Piggy Pink!" said Jessica Finch.

"Mud," said Brad.

"Moody Blue!" said Judy.

When they were finished, Ms. Tater let them ask questions.

"How long does it take to make a crayon?" asked Jessica Finch.

"About fifteen minutes."

"How long does it take to write a book?" asked Rocky.

"A lot longer than that. It took me about one year."

"Who invented crayons anyway? George Washington?" asked Frank.

"Well," said Ms. Tater, "two guys named Binney and Smith made the first crayon. It was black. Mr. Binney's wife, Alice, was a teacher, like Mr. Todd. She invented the name Crayola."

"Any more questions?" asked Mr. Todd.

Judy waved her hand in the air. "I have a comment, not a question."

"Yes?" said Ms. Tater.

"You were so non-boring."

"Thank you," Ms. Tater said. "What a great compliment."

Everybody clapped for the Crayon Lady when the program was over.

"Okay, 3T," said Mr. Todd, "Ms. Tater brought free crayons for all of us. Line up and I'll pass them out. Then you can go back to your seats and draw."

Judy got in line for her crayon. That's when she saw it. The candle! All the wax from the candle that Ms. Tater lit had dripped to one side. The left side.

But wait! If Mr. Todd was in love, the candle would have dripped to the *right* side. The left side meant a *woman* was in love.

Judy looked harder at the Crayon Lady. Mr. Todd handed her a Vermilion Red crayon. Ms. Tater smiled back at him like he had just turned into a handsome prince or something.

Or something! *Boing!* Of course! That was it! Ms. Tater was in love! The candle drips proved it. Judy saw it with her own eyes. And *Tater* started with *T*. Just like the apple seed said.

At last, she, Judy Moody, had made a *non*-fiction prediction! Mr. Todd was in love with the Crayon Lady! The Crayon Lady was in love with Mr. Todd. There were a Vermilion and one reasons.

Purple Mountain Majesty

Judy Moody was in a tell-the-world mood.
Judy told Frank Pearl. Judy told Rocky and
Stink and the whole bus. Judy told Mom
and Dad when she got home. She even
called Jessica Finch. She announced to the
whole world her best-ever, foretell-the-
future, *non*-fiction prediction: "Madame M
predicts . . . Twa la! Mr. Todd and the
Crayon Lady are in love!"

      ☙   ☙   ☙

By the next morning, Virginia Dare School was buzzing with the news. Really and truly? Could it be? Had Judy Moody predicted the future, once and for all? How did she know? Should they ask Mr. Todd?

That morning, Class 3T sat about as still as popping popcorn.

"My, aren't we jumpy this morning," said Mr. Todd.

"We have something we want to ask you," said Judy. She added three new bite marks to her pencil.

"Yes, yes, yes," everybody agreed.

"Well, before you ask me your question, I have some important news to tell all of you. It's a secret, but I think it's time I let you in on it."

Chomp, chomp. Judy chewed on her pencil eraser.

"You know Ms. Tater, the author you met yesterday?"

Judy nearly choked on her pencil eraser! The whole class seemed to hold its breath. The popcorn stopped popping.

"I hope you enjoyed her presentation, and I hope you all learned something about making crayons and something about making books."

Bite, bite. Chomp.

"I told you Ms. Tater is a special friend. And I'm so glad you all had a chance to meet her, because Ms. Tater and I are engaged. We are going to be married! And you are all invited to our wedding."

"Wedding!" "Mmm, cake!" "Can I come?" "When?" "Will you still be our teacher?"

Questions and more questions zoomed around the room.

"Will there be a lot of crayons at your house?" asked Jessica Finch.

"Will your kids be the Tater-Todds?" asked Frank. He cracked himself up.

Judy did not even stop to laugh. "I KNEW IT!" She jumped right out of her seat. Her bite-mark pencil flew to the front of the room. She practically did a dance right in the middle of the second row from the right.

"Judy Moody predicted it!" yelled Frank Pearl. "She was right!"

"She knew yesterday!" said Rocky. "She told us on the bus."

"She called me!" said Jessica Finch.

Everybody pointed to Judy. "She did! She told us! She knew! She predicted it right!"

"Judy," said Mr. Todd, "is this true?"

"It's *non*-fiction," said Judy.

"How did you know? We thought we had a pretty good secret."

Judy thought of all the ways she knew. The mood ring turning red. The apple seed. The candle wax. But most of all it was the way Mr. Todd smiled ear to ear around Ms. Tater. And the way Ms. Tater's eyes looked when she showed them the Pumpkin Moon crayon.

She could say it was the mood ring. She

could say it was ESP. She could say that she, Madame M for Moody, saw the future. Just like Jeane Dixon, Famous American Fortuneteller, without the eggs. But Judy realized — some things you just know. In your heart. There's no explaining them.

"How I knew is a secret," said Judy.

       ⊚   ⊚   ⊚

At last, she, Judy Moody, had predicted the future.

As soon as she got home, Judy ran straight to her room, opened up her super-special baby-tooth box, and took out her mood ring. Judy slipped the mood ring onto her finger. She closed her eyes. She held her breath. She counted to eight, her favorite number. She thought of purple things: cool arm slings and dragonfly wings, grape bubblegum and not-pond-scum mood rings.

At last, Judy opened her eyes.

Black! The mood ring was black as Christmas-stocking coal. Black as a bad-luck ink splat. Black as a bad mood.

How could it be black when she was On-Top-of-Spaghetti happy? No, wait! The mood ring was changing. Yes. Right before her eyes. The mood ring turned purple! Mountain Majesty Purple! No lie. She, Judy Moody, was in a *Joyful, On-Top-of-the-World* mood.

Mr. Todd said that everybody played a part in their own future, and the future was looking brighter already. From now on, Judy would take the future into her own hands, and there was no time like the present to get started.

She took out a non-Grouchy pencil and she wrote some non-fiction in her non-homework journal.

Judy Moody's Plans for the Future

Spell tortilla and zigzag the right way.
Get Stink to stop bugging me.
Maybe write a book (not about crayons).
Paint my room Purple Mountain Majesty.
Dress up fancy for a wedding.
Become a doctor?

The future was out there, waiting. And there was one more thing Judy did know for sure and absolute positive — there would be many more moods to come.

Megan McDonald ────────

is the award-winning author of the Judy Moody series. She says that most of Judy's stories "grew out of anecdotes about growing up with my four sisters." She confesses, "I *am* Judy Moody. Same-same! In my family of sisters, we're famous for exaggeration. Judy Moody is me . . . exaggerated." Megan McDonald lives with her husband in northern California.

Peter H. Reynolds ────────

says he felt an immediate connection to Judy Moody because, "having a daughter, I have witnessed firsthand the adventures of a very independent-minded girl." Peter H. Reynolds lives in Massachusetts, just down the street from his twin brother.

Praise for Judy Moody Predicts the Future

A New York Book Show Merit Award Winner

"The irrepressible Judy is completely believable."
— *Booklist*

"Established fans and new readers will enjoy this
adventure. Amusing black-and-white watercolors
capture the humor and the girl's inimitable spirit.
Prediction: another winner starring Judy Moody."
— *School Library Journal*

Be sure to read Judy's next adventure!

DOUBLE RARE!
Judy Moody has her own website!

Come visit **www.judymoody.com**
for the latest in all things Judy Moody, including:

- ◉ All you need to know about the best-ever Judy Moody Fan Club

- ◉ Answers to all your V.I.Q.s (very important questions) about Judy

- ◉ Way-not-boring stuff about Megan McDonald and Peter H. Reynolds

- ◉ Double-cool activities that will be sure to put you in a mood—and not a bad mood, a good mood!

- ◉ Totally awesome T.P. Club info!

Hey, don't forget about me! find out about my books and learn how to make your own comics at www.stinkmoody.com.

Look out, Judy Moody!

StinK

is starring in
his very own series!

#1

Stink The Incredible Shrinking Kid

Megan McDonald

#2

Stink and the Incredible Super-Galactic Jawbreaker

Megan McDonald

illustrated by Peter H. Reynolds

Be sure to check out
Stink's adventures!

Experience
all of
Judy Moody's
moods!

Judy MOOdy, M.D.
The Doctor IS In!

Alia Irizarry
Ortiz

Books by Megan McDonald and Peter H. Reynolds:

#1 – *Judy Moody*

#2 – *Judy Moody Gets Famous!*

#3 – *Judy Moody Saves the World!*

#4 – *Judy Moody Predicts the Future*

#5 – *Judy Moody, M.D.: The Doctor Is In!*

#6 – *Judy Moody Declares Independence*

#1 – *Stink: The Incredible Shrinking Kid*

#2 – *Stink and the Incredible Super-Galactic Jawbreaker*

The Judy Moody Mood Journal

Judy Moody's Double-Rare Way-Not-Boring Book of Fun Stuff to Do

Books by Megan McDonald:

Ant and Honey Bee: What a Pair!

The Sisters Club

Books by Peter H. Reynolds:

The Dot

Ish

Judy MOOdy, M.D.
The Doctor IS In!

Megan McDonald

illustrated by
PeteR H. Reynolds

CANDLEWICK PRESS
CAMBRIDGE, MASSACHUSETTS

First paperback edition 2006

The Library of Congress has cataloged the hardcover edition as follows:

McDonald, Megan.
Judy Moody, M.D. : The doctor is in! ; illustrated by Peter H. Reynolds.
—1st ed.
p.   cm.
Summary: Judy is all excited about becoming a doctor, especially when
Class 3T starts a new unit on the human body, but she learns more about
being a patient when she catches tonsillitis from her little brother, Stink.
ISBN 978-0-7636-2024-0 (hardcover)
[1. Sick—Fiction. 2. Medical care—Fiction. 3. Brothers—Fiction.
4. Schools—Fiction. 5. Humorous stories.] I. Reynolds, Peter, date, ill. II. Title.
PZ7.M1487Jp 2004
[Fic]—dc22   2003055336

ISBN 978-0-7636-2615-0 (paperback)

8 10 9 7

Printed in the United States of America

This book was typeset in Stone Informal and Judy Moody.
The illustrations were done in watercolor, tea, and ink.

Candlewick Press
2067 Massachusetts Avenue
Cambridge, Massachusetts 02140

visit us at www.candlewick.com

For my editor, Mary Lee Donovan,
who cheerfully helps with Moody Days,
Multiple Deadlines, Melt-Downs,
and other Mega-Disasters.

M.M.

To Maribeth Bush, whose "can do"
spirit inspires so many!

P.H.R.

Table of Contents

M.D. = A Moody Day 1

M.D. = MeDullas and ManDibles 9

M.D. = Mystery Detective 23

M.D. = A Million Dollars 37

M.D. = Mucus Dermis 48

M.D. = Mr. DryBones 55

M.D. = Majorly Delicious! 69

M.D. = Medical Doctor 84

M.D. = Medical Disaster 102

M.D. = Mumpty Dumpty 120

M.D. = Most Definitely 136

Judy

First Girl Doctor

Who's

Dad

Father of Mumpty Dumpty

Mom

Nurse-in-Residence

Mouse

Cool Critter

Stink

Organ donor

Who

Rocky

Judy's new
un-best friend

Toady

Guinea pig?

Mr. Todd

For pencil emergencies,
dial Mr. Todd.

Frank

Gene-ius

Jessica

Diagnosis:
Cooties on the
medulla

M.D. = A Moody Day

PLIP! Judy Moody woke up. *Drip, drip, drip* went rain on the roof. *Blip, blip, blip* went drops on the window. Not again! It had been raining for seven days straight. Bor-ing!

She, Judy Moody, was sick and tired of rain.

Judy put her head under the pillow. If only she was sick. Being sick was the greatest. You got to stay home and drink pop for breakfast and eat toast cut in special strips and watch TV in your room. You got to read Cherry Ames, Student Nurse, mysteries all day. And you got to eat yummy cherry cough drops. Hey! Maybe Cherry Ames was named after a cough drop!

Judy took out her mom's old Cherry Ames book and popped a cough drop in her mouth anyway.

"Get up, Lazybones!" said Stink, knocking on her door.

"Can't," said Judy. "Too much rain."

"What?"

"Never mind. Just go to school without me."

"Mom, Judy's skipping school!" Stink yelled.

Mom came into Judy's room. "Judy, honey. What's wrong?"

"I'm sick. Of *rain*," she whispered to Mouse.

"Sick? What's wrong? What hurts?" asked Mom.

"My head, for one thing. From all that noisy rain."

"You have a headache?"

"Yes. And a sore throat. And a fever. And a stiff neck."

"That's from sleeping with the diction-ary under your pillow," said Stink. "To ace your spelling test."

"Is not."

"Is too!"

"See, look. My tongue's all red." Judy

stuck out her Cherry-Ames-cough-drop tongue at Stink.

Mom felt Judy's head. "You don't seem to have a fever."

"Faker," said Stink.

"Come back in five minutes," said Judy. "I'll have a fever by then."

"Faker, faker, faker," said Stink.

If only she had measles. Or chicken pox. Or . . . MUMPS! Mumps gave you a headache. Mumps gave you a stiff neck and a sore throat. Mumps made your cheeks stick out like Humpty Dumpty. Judy pushed the cough drop into her cheek and made it stick out, Humpty-Dumpty style.

"Mumps!" said Dr. Judy. "I think I have the mumps! For real!"

"Mumps!" said Stink. "No way. You got a shot for that. A no-mumps shot. We both did. Didn't we, Mom?"

"Yes," said Mom. "Stink's right."

"Maybe one mump got through."

"Sounds like somebody doesn't want to go to school today," said Mom.

"Can I? Can I stay home, Mom? I promise I'll be sick. All day."

"Let's take your temperature," said Mom. She took the thermometer out of the case.

"Cat hair?" said Mom. "Is this cat hair on the thermometer?"

"She's always making Mouse stick out her tongue and taking the cat's temperature," said Stink.

Mom shook her head and went to wash off the thermometer. When she came back, she took Judy's temperature. "It's 98.6," said Mom. "Normal!"

"Faker, fakey, not-sick, big fat faker," said Stink.

"At least my temperature's normal," said Judy. "Even if my brother isn't."

"Better get dressed," said Mom. "Don't want to be late."

"Stink? You're a rat fink. Stink Rat-Fink Moody. That's what I'll call you from now on."

"Well, you'll have to call me it at school 'cause you don't get to stay home."

Judy stuck out her cherry-red, no-mumps tongue at Stink.

She was down in the dumps. She had a bad case of the grumps. The no-mumps Moody Monday blues. She, Judy Moody, felt like Mumpty Dumpty! Mumpty Dumpty without a temperature, that is.

M.D. = MeDullas and ManDibles

When Judy walked into Class 3T (seven minutes late!) on the un-mumpsy day of Monday, Class 3T was dry as a bone. Or bones! There were bones everywhere.

Mr. Todd had made a new bulletin board: *Our Amazing Body: From Head to Toe*. It had a tall poster of bones with long scientific names. On the front board he taped a chart that showed rodent bones. It looked like the insides of Peanut, the dwarf guinea pig in Class 3T. And . . . sitting behind Mr. Todd's desk in Mr. Todd's chair, using Mr. Todd's pencil, was a glow-in-the-dark skeleton!

Class 3T had turned into a bone museum!

Bones were not drippy. Bones were not noisy. Bones were not boring. Bones were dry and quiet and very, very interesting!

Things were sure looking up for a no-mumps Monday. Judy handed Mr. Todd her late slip. "Sorry I'm late," she said. "I almost had the mumps."

"Well, I'm glad you're healthy, and here now. We're starting a new unit on the Human Body from head to toe."

"We're going to get to jump rope," said

Jessica Finch. "And measure our heart rates."

"And play Twister," said Rocky. "To learn about muscles."

"And sing a song about bones," said Alison S.

"I can't believe you started the human body without me!" said Judy. "A person can miss a lot in seven minutes."

"Don't worry. I think you'll catch up," said Mr. Todd.

Mr. Todd taught them a funny song that went, "Da foot bone's connected to da ankle bone. . . ." He read them a book called *Frozen Man,* the incredible, real-life story of a five-thousand-year-old mummy.

And Class 3T got to turn out the lights and use the glow-in-the-dark skeleton named Bonita to count how many bones were in a human. Two hundred and six!

"We'll be learning a lot of new words in this unit. The scientific names for bones and body parts come from Latin. So they may sound a little funny."

"Like *maxilla* is your jaw?" asked Judy, looking at the bulletin board.

"And so is *mandible*," said Jessica.

Jessica Finch had already learned to spell *microbes* (a fancy word for germs, as in cooties!) and *medulla* (a fancy word for brain stuff). "Can you spell *headache*?" Judy asked. Frank Pearl cracked up at that one.

Then Mr. Todd passed out owl pellets. They got to poke them with a pencil to find bones. Rodent bones. Judy and Frank stared at their fuzzy gray lump.

"Double bluck! Just think. This is owl spit-up!" said Frank.

"It's still interesting," said Judy. "Real bones are in there. Skulls and stuff."

"You poke it," said Frank. So Judy poked it with her Grouchy pencil. They found a jawbone, a rib, and a bone Mr. Todd called a *femur*. They glued each bone onto paper and drew in all the missing bones to make a rodent skeleton that matched the one on the board.

"Do any rodent bones have the same names as human bones?" asked Mr. Todd.

Judy raised her hand.

"Tibia," called out Jessica Finch.

"Very good," said Mr. Todd.

"That's what I was going to say," said Judy. Jessica Finch was a rat fink (like Stink!) for not raising her hand. A *rodent* fink.

"Now let's talk about your Human Body projects," said Mr. Todd. "Projects will be due in two weeks. You can do your project on bones, muscles, joints, the brain —"

"Even toenails?" asked Bradley.

"As long as it teaches us something about the human body. Let's start by writing down ideas in your notebooks. I want to see brainstorming."

□ Do an operation (on Toady?)

□ Dress up and be Elizabeth Blackwell (first woman doctor)

□ Tell doctor jokes about body parts

□ Show and Tell a body part (from scab collection)

□ Listen to heart beat with stethoscope

Judy had a storm in her brain already.

Rocky wanted to do three-thousand-year-old human body stuff. Mummies!

"What are you thinking of doing?" Judy asked Frank.

"Cloning. I'll be a fiction scientist or a science fictiontist. Somebody who clones stuff. Like in *Jurassic Park*. They used a drop of mosquito blood and made a whole dinosaur. They do it in real life, too. Start with one cell, like from your DNA, and make a whole new you."

"*Double* cool!" Judy said.

"I'm going to write a dictionary," Jessica told Judy. "With human body words like *appendix* and *patella*. That's your knee." Jessica Finch had *cooties* on the *medulla* if she thought she could rewrite the dictionary.

Judy looked back at her own paper. She chewed her eraser. She chewed her fingernail. She chewed her hair. Judy had a brain wave! A real-body-parts idea. She would call Grandma Lou to see if she had any good body parts for Showing and Telling. Something better than scabs. This was the brainiest of all storms! She wrote down *Call Grandma Lou* so she wouldn't forget.

Judy's just-sharpened Grouchy pencil was still flying when Mr. Todd said, "Class, that's enough brainstorming for today."

"Good. My brain hurts," said Frank.

"I'm passing out permission slips for our field trip."

Field trip! "Is it to Screamin' Mimi's?" asked Judy. "Please, please, pretty please with chocolate mud ice cream on top?"

"Max and Kelsey's dad, from Class 3M, works at the hospital. So we're invited to go with their class to the Walter Reed Memorial Hospital emergency room. We'll learn all about the human body and get to see people who make a difference *in action.*"

Emergency room! That was even better than Screamin' Mimi's! Judy Moody dropped her *mandible!* And her Grouchy pencil.

"I was there when I broke my finger,"

said Frank, waving his crooked pinkie. "They have a nurse named Ron."

"I went when my brother stuck a Lego up his nose," said Bradley.

"Can we go see all the new babies?" asked Frank. "They're so wrinkly."

"Well, I'm glad the whole class is enthusiastic," said Mr. Todd.

"When do we go? When? When?" everybody asked.

"Monday. One week from today. Dr. Nosier will be giving us a tour."

"Dr. Nosehair!" said Rocky, and everybody cracked up.

She, Judy Moody, and Class 3T were going to the ER. For real and absolute positive. The blood-and-guts, real-body-parts emergency room.

Judy reached down to pick up her Grouchy pencil. The tip was broken. "Mr. Todd," she asked, "may I please sharpen my pencil?"

"Remember what we said about sharpening pencils ten times a day?"

"But Mr. Todd," said Judy, "it's an emergency."

"What?"

"A *pencil* emergency! My pencil just broke its spinal cord!" said Judy.

Emergency

M.D. = Mystery Detective

The next Monday was a better-than-best-ever third grade day. At lunch, Judy ate her PBJ sandwich in seven bites, then walked-not-ran to the playground. Class 3T had a ten-minute recess before their field trip to the hospital.

Judy's mom was a driver and parent volunteer, so Rocky and Frank rode in their car. Mom made Judy ask Jessica Finch, too.

"Did you know *muscle* comes from a

word that means mouse?" asked Jessica. "If you move a muscle, it looks like a mouse." She flexed her arm.

Judy used all forty-three muscles it took to frown at Jessica Finch.

⊚   ⊚   ⊚

At the hospital, Dr. Nosehair led Class 3T down a long hall.

"Why does that doctor lady have a rabbit?" asked Frank.

"Animals aren't allowed in the hospital!" said Jessica.

"It's a new program called Paws for Healing," Dr. Nosier told them. "People bring animals to patients in the hospital to help them feel better. Holding an animal and petting it can actually lower a person's blood pressure, and help a patient forget about being sick."

"RARE!" said Judy.

Dr. N. took them into a room in back of the ER, where Class 3M was already waiting. There were lots of machines. And important-looking stuff.

"What's the first thing you would do in an emergency?" quizzed Dr. Nosier.

"Call 911!" everybody said.

"Would you call 911 to find out how long to cook a turkey?"

"Only if *you're* a turkey," Frank said. Judy and Frank cracked up.

"Is a crossword puzzle an emergency?"

"Only for my dad, who tries to beat the clock," said Judy.

"Believe it or not, we do get people who call 911 for such things. But let's say we have a real emergency, like a car accident or a heart attack. Everything around here happens super fast. As soon as the ambulance arrives, the EMTs, people trained to handle medical emergencies, start 'giving the bullet,'—telling us what happened. *Train wreck* means the patient has lots of things wrong with them. Who knows what *code blue* means?"

"Lots of blood?"

"All the people in blue shirts have to help?"

"It means somebody's heart stopped," said Dr. Nosier.

"You fix hearts that stop?" asked Alison S.

"You must help a lot of people!" said Erica.

"All doctors make a promise to help people. It's called the Hippocratic oath. Hippocrates was the Father of Medicine. In the old days, you had to swear by Apollo and Hygeia to help people the best you could. If you didn't know what was wrong with a patient, you had to say 'I know not.' The old oath sounds funny to us now, so a doctor named Louis Lasagna rewrote it."

"Louis *Lasagna*? Did he invent pizza, too?" asked Frank. Dr. N. laughed.

"But how do you always know what to do?" asked Rocky.

"Being a doctor is like being a detective. You look at all the clues and try to solve the mystery. In the ER we just do it in a hurry. Think of it like each one of us is a human jigsaw puzzle. My job is to figure out the missing pieces and put the puzzle back together."

"RARE!" whispered Judy.

"I'm the best at jigsaw puzzles," bragged Jessica Finch. "I did a five-hundred-piece jigsaw puzzle of Big Ben all by myself!" Sometimes Judy wished Jessica Finch would shut her *mandible*.

"Now I'll show you what some of this stuff is for," said Dr. Nosier. Dr. Judy got to use a stethoscope to listen to her own heartbeat! *Ba-boom, ba-boom!* Then she took Frank's blood pressure (for real!), looked for Jessica Finch's tonsils, and saw eye insides with a special kind of scope. They took turns riding on a bed called a gurney, walking with crutches, and sitting in a wheelchair.

Dr. N. turned out all the lights and showed them x-rays. There was a brain (it looked all ghosty), a dog that got hit by a car (it looked all sideways), even a violin (it looked all dead!). "X-rays help solve the mystery," he said.

They even got to see a real live, ooey-gooey heart on a TV. "This is better than the Operation Channel at home!" Judy said.

And they got to practice on life-size dummies called Hurt-Head Harry and Trauma Tammy. "I have a practice doll, too," said Judy. "With three heads. Hedda-Get-Betta. I practice being a doctor, like Elizabeth Blackwell."

"How would you like to practice being a patient with a broken arm?" asked Dr. N. "And I'll show everybody how we put on a cast."

Judy Moody could not believe her inner, middle, or outer ears. "Can I, Mom?"

"Sure, if you want to."

"Hold out your arm, Judy Moody, First Girl Doctor."

Judy grinned with all seventeen muscles it takes to make a smile. She held her arm out straight as a snowman's stick-arm. Dr. N. wrapped it around and around with soft cotton stuff.

"I'll use a special plaster bandage that turns hard when it dries so Judy won't be able to move that arm. That way her bone will stay in place and heal back together."

"My *radius* or my *ulna*?" asked Judy.

"I see you know your bones! Can you still wiggle your *phalanges*?"

Judy wiggled her fingers. Everybody laughed.

"A not-broken arm is even better than a

broken arm! I wish I never had to take it off."

"Tell you what," said Dr. Nosier. "If your mom says it's okay, you can wear it home. I'll show her how to take it off."

"Can I, Mom? Can I? I can fool Stink! Please, pretty please with Band-Aids on top?"

"I don't see why not," said Mom. "Sure!"

"RARE!" said Judy. She, Judy Moody, was a mystery. A human jigsaw puzzle with a broken arm . . . NOT!

Judy was so happy from Hospital Day that even her eyebrows were smiling. She stared at all the autographs on her cast. Even Dr. Nosehair had signed it. His autograph looked like a messy blob, but still!

She could hardly wait to get home and show Dad her cast. Maybe she could even get out of setting the table, on account of her broken arm (not!). Wait till she told Stink!

When she got home, Stink was waiting at the front door. Judy held up her cast.

"You broke your arm?" asked Stink. "Sweet!"

M.D. = A Million Dollars

She, Judy Moody, was in an operating mood! As soon as she got her cast off, Judy asked Stink to play Operation, a game where you remove body parts with tweezers and try NOT to make the buzzer go off.

Dr. Judy performed a delicate operation and removed butterflies from the patient's stomach. Next she removed his broken heart. Stink went for the charley horse. *Buzz!* "Hey, his nose lights up red," he said.

"Like Rudolph the Red-Nosed Reindeer!"

"You did that on purpose!"

"Did not!" Stink tried to remove the pencil from the guy's arm, to get rid of writer's cramp. *Buzz! Buzz! Buzz!*

"Stink. Give me the tweezers. Your turn's over when you buzz."

"Let's play something else," said Stink.

"I know," Judy said. "You can help me with my Human Body project for school."

"That's not playing. That's homework," said Stink.

"*Fun* homework," said Judy. "I'm going to do an operation with real stitches and stuff." Judy got out her doctor kit. "All I need is somebody to operate on."

"You're not operating on me. Just so you

know. No slings or eye patches or anything."

"Can I at least take your blood pressure?"

"I guess." Judy put a cuff around Stink's arm and pumped air into it. "I'm afraid you have high blood pressure, Stink," said Judy. "Your heart's beating super fast."

"That's 'cause I'm scared of what you might do to me!"

"I have a better idea." Judy went straight to Toady's aquarium. "Operation Toady! You hold him down, Stink, and I'll make the incision."

"The what?"

"The cut. Hel-lo? It's an *oper-a-tion*."

"You're loony tunes!" Stink said. "You can't cut Toady open."

"I'll stitch him back up. C'mon. Just one small, teensy- weensy snip?"

"N-O, no! Give me him!"

"It's the only way to see toad insides. Admit it, Stink. You want to see toad guts."

"Not *this* toad's guts." Stink rushed over to his desk and rooted around in the top drawer. He held up a cardboard badge that said ASPCA: SAVING LIVES SINCE 1866.

"Busted!" said Stink, holding the badge up to Judy's face. "It's against the law to be mean to animals or hurt them. Ever. Just show them respect and kindness. You're not even supposed to let your dog drink out of the toilet."

"I don't have a dog. And Mouse doesn't drink out of the toilet!"

"Good. If she did, you'd go to jail."

"I was just going to practice on Toady. Not put him in the toilet!"

"You're not allowed to test stuff out on animals. You're supposed to test on beans. Or pumpkins. People who make soap and shampoo and underpants and stuff are always testing it on animals, and the animals get hurt or even die."

"Stink, nobody makes animals wear underpants."

"Yah-huh. They do. No lie. It makes me really sad and mad that people do stuff to animals. I'm so sad and so mad I'm . . . smad!"

"Okay, okay! Don't be smad. I cross-my-heart promise I won't shampoo Toady or make him wear underpants or anything. I just wish I had something really good for Sharing tomorrow. Something nobody's ever seen. Something *human*."

"Like what?"

"Like Einstein's brain. A hair from Abraham Lincoln's beard. Or Grandma Lou's kidney stone, if only she had saved it."

"Put a kidney bean in a jar and say it's Einstein's brain. You could say it's a human bean, get it?"

"Hardee-har-har, Stink."

"I have some baby teeth. Teeth are human."

"Everybody's seen baby teeth, Stink."

"I have a toenail collection."

"Bor-ing."

"Wait! I *do* have a body part."

"What? What is it? Can I have it?"

"Nope. I'm not showing you 'cause you'll want it bad."

"Is it a finger? Or an ear?"

"NO!"

"A bone?"

"Nope."

"Is it skin? Like you peel off when you get sunburned?"

"Nope."

"Is it a cavity? You know, like in a tooth?"

"Nope."

"C'mon, Stinker. You HAVE to show me."

"Okay, but promise you won't SHOW or TELL anybody, and you can't take it to school, okay?"

"Cross-my-heart promise," said Judy. Stink went over to his closet. He pulled down a dusty box from the shelf. A box with all his baby stuff.

"Hurry up. I can't stand it!" said Judy. Stink opened the box and took out a baby-food jar. There was something in the jar. Something that looked like a shriveled-up, shrunken dead worm.

"Yee-uck. What is it? A petrified worm? Or one-hundred-year-old burnt spaghetti?"

"No, Einstein. It's my bellybutton!"

"Your bellybutton?"

"You know. That thing that falls off your bellybutton when you're born."

"For real and true?"

"Yes, for real. When Mom brought me home from the hospital—"

"But you were born in a Jeep!"

"You know what I mean. When I came home, I had a thing on my bellybutton. You have to wait for it to fall off. Mom said you wanted to keep it."

"Me? So, then, really it's mine?"

"NO! It's *my* body part. I used to be an outie. Now I'm an innie." Stink lifted up his shirt. "See?"

"RARE!" said Judy. "I can't wait for my class"— Stink gave her a starey, glarey look — "to NOT know about this. Ever."

Stink put the jar with his wormy old burnt-spaghetti bellybutton on the desk. "You know what's so great about this belly-button?"

"What?" asked Judy.

"That you don't have one!" said Stink. He laughed himself silly. "But if you give me a million dollars, I'll let you take my bellybutton to school."

"How about five dollars?"

"A million dollars or you'll never, not ever, touch my bellybutton!" said Stink.

M.D. = Mucus Dermis

Wednesday. Wednesday was her Sharing Day! Judy was going to have the best share ever. She couldn't wait two weeks until her Human Body project was due. She, Judy Moody, would Show and Tell about Stink's bellybutton. To-day. All she had to do was steal it.

Judy waited for Stink to go downstairs for breakfast. She tiptoed into his room, took down the box of baby stuff, grabbed

Stink's bellybutton jar, and hid it in the secret inside pocket of her backpack.

@   @   @

As soon as the bell rang, Mr. Todd asked Class 3T to form a Sharing Circle. It was Rocky's day to share, too. And Jessica Finch. Jessica said she'd brought an especially special share. But Judy just knew her belly-button had to be the specialest!

Rocky went first. His share was a Lego. Judy thought one Lego was boring, until Rocky conducted an experiment on it. He put it in a petri dish and poured some stuff on it. The Lego turned black-as-dirt from all the germs on it.

"Eee-yew!" said Jessica Finch. "Germs!" Germs made her squirm.

"There's a fungus among us," said Frank.

"I had lice before," said Bradley. "In my hair!"

"Me too!" said Alison S.

"Ick," said Dylan, backing away from the circle.

"Millions of bacteria are on us all the time," said Rocky. "On our heads, up our noses, between our toes."

"That's right," said Mr. Todd. "Each one of us is our own ecosystem. We carry around millions of critters too tiny to see."

"Like a human rain forest?" asked Judy.

"Exactly," said Mr. Todd. "Now do you see why I'm always after all of you to wash your hands?"

"I have something that's not germs,"
Jessica said. "My guinea pig, Chester, was
a boy, but he turned out to be a girl and
had babies." Jessica Finch held up a picture. "Nutmeg, Jasmine, Coco, and Cindy,
short for Cinnamon. The Spice Girls!"

"Aww!" everybody said. "Cute!" Judy took a look. All she could see were hairballs. Bellybuttons were way more scientific than hairballs!

"Judy, did you bring anything to share?" asked Mr. Todd.

"Yes," said Judy. She held the baby-food jar behind her back. "See, when you're a baby and you first come out, there's a thingy attached to your bellybutton. Then it falls off and your mom and dad find out if you're an innie or an outie."

"I'm an innie!" said Frank.

"Ooh. I'm a way-outie!" said Bradley, showing off his bellybutton.

"Okay, 3T! Keep your shirts on," said Mr. Todd. "Let's let Judy finish."

"In this jar, I have a real live bellybutton thingy. No lie. I call it *Mucus Dermis*. It's Latin. *Dermis* means skin and *mucus* means yucky. Yucky skin."

"Where'd you get it?" asked Rocky.

"Actually, it's from my very own brother, Stink Moody."

"Double yuck," said Jessica Finch, squirming in a wormy way.

"Let me see!" said Frank Pearl. Judy passed Stink's bellybutton to Frank Pearl. Everybody crowded around to see.

"Take your seats and Judy will pass it around," said Mr. Todd.

"Bellybuttons are also called navels," said Judy. "Everybody has one, but no two are alike. Just like snowflakes. Sometimes bellybuttons collect lint, and in Japan, they have bellybutton cleaners. My dad told me. No lie!"

"Thank you, Judy," said Mr. Todd. "I think we've all learned more than we ever imagined about bellybuttons."

"Bellybuttons are better than bones," said Rocky.

"Better than lice!" said Frank.

"Better than hairballs!" said Judy.

"Does your brother know you have his bellybutton?" asked Jessica.

M.D. = Mr. DryBones

After Sharing, Judy went out in the hall to put away her backpack. Stink was there, listening right outside the classroom.

"Give it," said Stink, holding out his hand.

"Give what?"

"I know you have it. I came to tell you . . . I just saw you! I overheard. . . . You stole it, didn't you? You showed the WHOLE ENTIRE WORLD my bellybutton!"

"Nah-uh! Only half of the third grade."

"You owe me a million dollars."

"Stink, we can fight later. Go back to second grade."

"I can't. I'm sick. My throat hurts. I think I have mumps."

"Made-up mumps?"

"No. For real." Stink held his neck like it really hurt.

"Would you say that the pain is in your *larynx* or your *pharynx*?" Judy asked.

"Huh?"

"Just go to the nurse," said Judy.

"I'm scared."

"Of what? Mrs. Bell?"

"No."

"A shot?"

"No."

"Getting lost?"

"No."

"For-real mumps? A pill? Throwing up?"

"No. No. And not really."

"What? What are you scared of?"

"The skeleton! In the nurse's office."

"Stink! It's not even real!"

Stink's face crumpled like he was going to cry. "The office lady told me to wait till Mrs. Bell gets here, but I was in there all by myself. With *it*."

"I'll take you, if you promise not to be mad about the bellybutton."

Judy got a pass from Mr. Todd, then walked Stink down the hall and around the corner to the nurse's office. Stink pointed to the skeleton in the corner.

"Pretend he's not there, Stink. Sit on the edge of the bed. I'll be the doctor while we wait for Mrs. Bell. So, what seems to be the problem?"

"When I woke up this morning, I just had hiccups and a loose tooth. Now my throat hurts."

Judy picked up a flashlight from the desk and shined it in Stink's eyes.

"Hey, now my eyes hurt, too!"

"Does your face hurt?"

"Nope."

"It's killing me!" Judy cracked herself up. "Let's see your throat." She shined the light down his throat. "Say ahh!"

"Glub!" said Stink.

"Not *glub. Ahhhhh!* Try again."

"Slug!"

"Never mind," said Judy.

"What's wrong?"

"Well, you DON'T have a frog in your throat. Just a glub and a slug." Judy held her head sideways, thinking. She looked Stink up and down.

"Do you have a pain in your neck, too?" asked Stink.

"Just you," said Judy. She cracked herself up some more. "Wait a minute! Stink! I got it! I know what you have!"

"What?" asked Stink.

"Skeleton-itis!" said Judy. "Fear-of-Skeletons disease. Found only in second graders with glubby slugs in their throats."

"I can't help it. He just stares . . . with those eyes! It's creepier than that pyramid eye on a one-dollar bill."

"Stink, skeletons don't have eyes."

"I know! Just big spooky holes like dead people. And he's all clickety-clackety."

Judy picked up the skeleton from where he was hanging in the corner. "Hi! I'm Mr. DryBones!" Judy clacked the skeleton's jaw open and shut. "You can call me George. See? He teaches you about your bones and stuff." Judy made the skeleton wave at Stink.

Stink did not wave back. "You're giving me goose bumps. Put him back before we get in trouble."

"Not till he tells some jokes. Here, I'll practice some jokes I'm learning for my Human Body project. Mr. DryBones likes jokes, don't you?" Judy said to the skeleton. "They tickle his *funny bone*!"

Stink cracked up.

"What does a skeleton take for a cold?" asked Judy.

"What?"

"Coffin drops!"

Stink laughed at that one.

"What do skeletons put on their mashed potatoes?"

"Umm . . ."

"Grave-y!"

"What do you call a skeleton who sleeps all day?"

"Sleepyhead?"

"Lazybones!" Judy cackled.

"How does a skeleton pass his math test?"

"How?"

"He bones up on his addition and subtraction."

"Fun-ny!" Stink laughed and laughed. He seemed to forget all about his sore throat. And Fear-of-Skeletons disease.

"What does a skeleton eat for breakfast?" asked Mrs. Bell, setting her purse down on the desk.

"I don't know? What?"

"Scream of wheat!"

"Good one!" said Stink. He held his stomach, he was laughing so hard.

"I see you've met George," said Mrs. Bell. "I had to go to another school this morning. So it's just my *skeleton* crew here today."

"Hey, that's good!" said Judy. "I was just, um, helping Stink until you got here."

"Old Mr. DryBones is very *humerus*," said Mrs. Bell. She cracked herself up. "*Humerus*. That's the name of this long bone right here in your upper arm."

"Cool beans!" said Judy.

"Oh, I get it now!" said Stink, cracking up too.

"See, Stink? I told you he wasn't scary."

"Don't worry," Mrs. Bell said to Stink. "Lots of people find bones scary. Did you know even elephants are afraid of bones?"

"Really?" asked Stink.

"Bones are interesting, really. We start out with over three hundred bones when we're born, and when we grow up we have—"

"Only two hundred and six!" said Judy. "We just learned that in Mr. Todd's class."

"How do we lose so many bones?" asked Stink.

"Some grow together," said Mrs. Bell. "To hold us up, make us strong. Otherwise we'd all be jellyfish. A jellyfish has no bones."

Judy went all limp, imitating a jellyfish. "See, Stink. Aren't you glad you're not a jellyfish?"

"No, because if I were, I could sting you!"

"So, what seems to be the problem, young man?" Mrs. Bell asked Stink.

"I have a stomachache."

"A stomachache?" said Judy. "I thought you had a sore throat."

"I do. But now my stomach hurts from laughing."

"So, I guess you could say your sister had you in *stitches,* huh?"

"Don't give her any ideas!" said Stink.

"Let's just take a look at that throat," said Mrs. Bell. "Say *aah!*"

"AHH!" said Stink.

"Hey! You didn't say *glub.* Or *slug,*" said Judy.

"Uh-oh," said Mrs. Bell. "Somebody's sick, all right."

"For real?" Judy asked. "Can I see?"

"His throat is as red as a fire engine." Mrs. Bell took Stink's temperature with a non-cat-hairy thermometer. "And he has a fever: 99.9."

"Stink, you have ALL the luck," said Judy.

M.D. = Majorly Delicious!

No fair! Stink got to go to the real doctor. Judy convinced her mom that she had to come too, so she could learn stuff.

Dr. McCavity looked in Stink's eyes and ears and down his throat with a purple tongue depressor. She explained how tonsils are two pink balls like grapes in back of your throat, and they can get infected with white specks and swell up and hurt.

Dr. McCavity told Mrs. Moody to give

Stink some special medicine and make sure he got lots of sleep. She told Stink to drink ginger ale and eat the Brat diet.

"He's been eating the brat diet since he was born!" Judy said.

Dr. McCavity laughed. "BRAT means Bananas, Rice, Applesauce, and Toast." She also told Stink to stay home from school till his fever was gone, and stay away from Judy as much as possible.

She really did say the last part!

"Just think," Judy told Stink. "If you get tonsillitis, you get to go to the hospital for an operation and get a bracelet with your name on it and wear funny pajamas and eat Popsicles all day."

"Well, let's hope it doesn't come to that,"

said Mom. "That would be a lot of Pop-sicles."

"We don't like to take out healthy ton-sils," said the doctor.

"But you said they were grapefruits," said Judy. "Maybe he has Grapefruit-itis!"

"Grapes," said Dr. McCavity. "Not grapefruit. If he takes care of those tonsils, he won't have to worry about Grapefruit-itis." She laughed again.

"Dr. McCavity, you should have been a dentist!" Judy cracked herself up.

"You like jokes? What did the doctor say to the patient with tonsillitis?"

"What?"

"Have a *swell* time!" said Dr. McCavity.

Double no fair! Stink got to stay home from school (for real), drink ginger ale (for breakfast), and eat mashed-banana toast all day (the bratty diet). AND he got to have TV in his room, even though Dr. McCavity did not say one thing about TV in your room.

Judy did not stay away from Stink as much as possible.

She took his temperature (way not normal) and made him a hospital bracelet with his name (Stinker) on it. She let him use her crazy straw to drink ginger ale. She read him Rex Morgan, M.D., comics and Cherry Ames, Student Nurse, mysteries.

She wrote him a prescription on her
doctor pad.

Stink Moody
Take two Popsicles and
call me in the morning.
— Dr. Judy Moody

She even took a Hippopotamus oath to
be nice to Stink. Nicey-nice. *Doctor* nice.

"Stink," she said, raising her right hand,
"I swear by Neopolitan and Hygiene and
Larry Lasagna that I will do everything I
can to the best of my ability to help make

you better. Here. Pet Mouse." She plopped Mouse on Stink's stomach.

"Ow!" said Stink. "She clawed me!" Mouse jumped to the floor.

Judy picked up Mouse again. "Stink, you have to pet her twenty times. It's called Paws for Healing. It will lower your blood pressure. Trust me."

"Are you sure it's not called Paws for Scratching?"

"Stink. Just try it." Judy plopped her cat on Stink again. Mouse bolted off the bed, knocking over the glass of ginger ale.

"Ahhh! Ginger ale! It's all over me," cried Stink.

Judy got Stink a towel. And a new ginger ale. And a clean crazy straw. She got him a not-wet blanket. She got him Baxter and Ebert, his stuffed-animal penguin and timber wolf.

@   @   @

For four days, she fed Toady. For four days, she brought Stink his homework. For four days, she watched *Megazoid and the Deltoid Bananas* with Stink, even though she wanted to watch the Operation Channel.

That's when she saw it. In an ad on TV not prescribed by Dr. McCavity. The one-and-only, for-sure cure for Stink.

"Are you tired all the time?"

Yes. Stink was sleeping right now!

"Are you sick? Want to be healthy? Live longer?"

Yes, yes, and YES!! Judy told the TV.

"We have a secret just for you. PRUNES!" said the cartoon lady on TV.

"PRUNES!" cried Judy. "UCK!"

"Bite them, chew them. Don't pooh-pooh them," said the TV lady. "CALIFORNIA PRUNES! The energy-packed super snack. Majorly delicious! Off to climb Mt. Everest? Take some PRUNES with you today."

Judy did not think Stink would be climbing Mt. Everest anytime soon. He could barely climb out of bed. But it was worth a try. All she had to do was convince Stink to eat one prune.

Judy tiptoed downstairs and opened the

kitchen cupboards. Tea bags, peanut butter, pretzels, crackers. . . . They had to be here somewhere. Judy pulled a chair over to the up-high cupboards. Ah-ha! A shiny bag!

Gravy?!

Gravy did not help you climb Mt. Everest. Gravy did not cure tonsils. Gravy did not make you live longer.

She spotted a yellow sun shining on the front of a pink and purple bag. Finally! Judy stared at two shriveled lumps. Prunes were icky. Sticky. Prunes were wrinkly as elephants and looked like one-hundred-and-fifty-year-old buffalo droppings. Two-hundred-year-old dried-up bellybuttons. Two-hundred-and-fifty-year-old tonsils.

Why do you have to eat bad stuff for good stuff to happen?

The world was backwards, according to Judy Moody.

Dr. Judy went back upstairs. "Stink! Wake up!" said Judy.

"Wha . . . ?"

"I have your cure! Right here in my hand. No more fever. No more grapefruit tonsils." Judy held out her hand. She showed Stink the prunes.

"What? What are those?" asked Stink.

"Prunes. The secret to not getting sick. The secret to climbing Mt. Everest."

"They look like moon rocks. Or petrified prune rocks."

"They do kind of look like the owl pellets we had in Science. . . ."

"Owl pellets! Owl pellets are hairballs. Owl pellets are spit-up."

"Prunes are just plums," said Judy. "C'mon. One bite."

"No way, Prunella De Vil. I am not eating a hairball. I am not eating spit-up."

"Don't you want to live longer? Don't you want to have teeny-tiny tonsils again?"

"Okay. Then help me. Say nice things about prunes," said Stink.

Judy sniffed a prune. "They don't smell like buffalo droppings."

"That's the nicest thing you can say about a prune?"

"They're not hairy."

"Not hairy is good," said Stink.

"I know," said Judy. "Close your eyes. On the count of three, we'll BOTH eat a prune at the same time.

"One, one thousand —"

Stink closed his eyes tight.

"Two, one thousand —"

Judy threw her prune in the trash.

"Three —"

Stink actually put the prune in his mouth.

"Eee-yew!" cried Stink. *Thwaaa!* Stink spit out the prune. It went flying across the floor and landed in a dust ball. "I licked it! It touched my taste buds!"

"It's supposed to taste MAJORLY delicious. The TV said so," Judy told him.

"It tastes majorly disgusting," said Stink. "You tricked me!"

"I was just trying to help you feel better," said Judy. "Now I'm a bad doctor and you'll *never* feel better."

"I feel better knowing I'm not going to eat that prune."

"Stink, don't you get it? That was the last prune. Now it has cat hair and spit all over it. What are we going to do?" Before you could say majorly dust ball, Mouse pounced on the cat-hairy spit-up prune.

"No! Mouse! Wait!" said Judy.

It was too late. *Ga-loomp!* Mouse chewed it up and swallowed. Hairball, spit, and all. Judy and Stink fell on the floor laughing.

Prune Lips licked her paws, face, and whiskers. "Mouse," said Judy, picking up her cat, "you are going to live a very long life."

"*Nine* long lives," said Stink.

M.D. = Medical Doctor

Doctor Day! The day Judy got to dress up like Elizabeth Blackwell, First Woman Doctor, and do a REAL LIVE operation for Class 3T. An operation was the best of all the brainstorms from her list. The best Human Body project ever. Better even than trying to doctor Stink.

Her patient was special. Her patient had green skin and did *not* talk back. Her patient would not hog the TV and drink all the ginger ale and spit out healthy prunes.

Her patient was perfect. She could hardly wait.

First she took one more bath.

Stink knocked on the bathroom door. "Knock-knock!"

"Who's there?"

"Stink, minus one bellybutton."

No answer.

"Mom! Judy's hogging the bathroom and she already took a million baths yesterday." Stink banged on the door. "Hurry up! I need to get in there!"

Judy came out with a towel on her head, and all-wrinkly hands and feet. "I liked it better when you were sick," said Judy.

"I liked it better when you didn't look like a spit-up prune," said Stink.

"Doctors have to be really, really clean, Stink. Elizabeth Blackwell took three cold showers a day!"

"Elizabeth Blackwell didn't leave a lake on the floor."

"Hardee-har-har."

"Hip bone's connected to da leg bone," Judy sang as she got dressed. Today was going to be the amazing-est human body day ever, from head to toe.

At school, Judy had ants in her pants all through Spelling, bees in her *patella*-knees all through Math. At last it was Science. Mr. Todd said the magic words. "Time for our

Human Body projects. Rocky, why don't you go first?"

Rocky wrapped himself in toilet paper like a mummy, and told how eating a mummy can help your tummy! No lie. Doctors in the old-old-olden days thought mummies could cure stuff like stomachaches. So they ground up mummies, bones and all, and used them for medicine.

"Creepy!" said most of the class.

"Fascinating," said Judy.

Jessica Finch wrote *medi-words*

on the board. Words like *intelligirl* (really smart girl), *brainiac* (has super-Einstein, not-kidney-bean brain), and *brain case* (sick in the brain), which she added to the dictionary. Then she passed out a word search. Judy found all the *medi-words* at *brainiac* speed.

Finally, Mr. Todd called on her. Dr. Judy Elizabeth Blackwell. She put on her doctor shirt, a stethoscope, and a left-eye patch. She taped plastic bags over her shoes. She colored between her eyebrows with a black marker and stuck fake bugs on her head with tape. "Today I am Elizabeth Blackwell, First Woman Doctor," said Judy. "I'll start with a poem." She took a deep breath, so

she wouldn't get a terrible case of nerves. Or
a bad case of sweat.

Elizabeth Blackwell

Lived in an attic
Nothing was automatic

First in her class
What more could you ask?

Became first woman doctor
Even though boys mocked her

Opened a clinic
Helped poor people in it

Delivered Babies
Gave shots for rabies (maybe)

Opened her own school
It was way cool

Wrote a book
Wonder how long it took.

Born, I don't know when
Died, 1910

Take after the example
Of Dr. Elizabeth Blackwell.

Everybody clapped. "Any questions before I begin the operation?" Judy asked.

"Why are you wearing pajamas?" asked Hailey.

"Scrubs," said Judy. "It's a doctor shirt. Doctors have to be really, really clean and take tons of baths a day."

"Why do you only have one eyebrow?" asked Frank.

"It's a uni-brow. Like Elizabeth Blackwell had. Plus it makes me look smart. Like an *intelligirl* who is not a *brain case.*"

"Why do you have that pirate patch on your eye?" asked Brad.

"Elizabeth Blackwell got an eye infection and they took out her eye, so she wore an eye patch."

"Ooh. Gross!"

"Why do you have fake bugs on your head?" asked Jessica Finch.

"They didn't really know how to fix her eye, so they put bloodsucking leeches on her head. They thought it would help."

"EEE-yew!" said a bunch of kids in the class.

"Did you write that poem?"

"Well, it wasn't a gnome!"

"Why do you have plastic bags on your feet?"

"In case of blood," said Judy.

"Class, let's let Judy show us her project," said Mr. Todd.

"Time for a real live operation!" said Judy.

"Do it on me!" said Frank.

"Not me!" said Rocky.

"If you need a guinea pig," said Jessica Finch, "do it on Peanut."

"I already have a patient."

"Is it dead?" asked Bradley.

"My patient is alive, not dead. My patient is better to practice on than a little brother. My patient has lots of guts. Ooey-gooey guts."

"Who is it?"

"Tell us!"

"Does it have a name?"

"Yes."

"Oh no! Does it have green skin?" asked Rocky.

"Yes!" said Judy.

"It's Toady!" Frank called out.

"Her name is . . . Ima," said Judy. She held up a zucchini with a Magic-Marker face. "Ima Green Zucchini!"

The whole class clapped.

Frank came up front to help. He held up Judy's x-ray drawing of the insides of a zucchini. "First, make sure you take an x-ray, so you know what you're doing."

"What's that big black blob?" asked Rocky.

"That's the thing I'm going to remove.

The appendix. Nobody really knows what the appendix is for, so it's a good thing to take out."

"I had my appendix out," said Alison S.

"I had mine out twice," said Bradley.

"Before you start," said Judy, "don't for-get to take the Hippo oath. Swear by the Hippo guy, Father of Medicine, and Mr. Clean and Louis Lasagna that you will do your doctor best. Then make sure the patient is clean."

Judy turned to Frank. "Toothbrush!" She scrubbed the zucchini with a toothbrush.

"Shot." Frank handed her the shot from her doctor kit.

"Give the patient a shot, so they fall asleep. Use your nicey-nicey voice and tell them they won't feel a thing. Or tell them a joke to make them feel okay. Like, what vegetable lives in a cage? A *zoo-chini*!"

Frank cracked up the most at that one.

"Knife!" Frank handed Judy a plastic knife.

"Next, make the incision."

"I-N-C-I-S-I-O-N," said Intelligirl Jessica Finch, Queen of Medi-words. "A cut, slash, or gash."

Judy poked the zucchini with the plastic knife.

"Scissors," said Judy. Frank handed her the scissors.

Snip, snip, snip.

"Blood!" Judy said to Frank. She pointed to the ketchup bottle. Frank poured ketchup all over the zucchini.

"Operations have lots of blood."

"All this ketchup stuff is making me hungry for hot dogs and stuff," said Rocky.

"Tweezers!" She whispered, "Clothes-pin" to Frank.

"Take out the appendix." Judy pulled out a hunk of seeds with the clothespin.

"Sponge!" Judy picked up the zucchini and wiped off the ketchup-blood. The zucchini was so ketchup-y, it slipped out of Judy's hands and fell to the floor.

OH, NO!

The kids in 3T leaned out of their seats to see what had happened. There, in the middle of aisle 3, was perfect patient Ima Green Zucchini, lying in a pool of ketchup-blood, broken in two!

"Rule number one: Stay calm," said Judy. "Admit 'I know not' what to do!"

Then she had an idea. Judy picked up both halves of her patient and said to Frank, "Sutures!" So Frank handed her a needle and some thread.

"I'll just sew the patient back up." Judy showed the class how to make nice neat stitches. *In, out, in, out.*

"Don't just do a *sew-sew* job. Or your patient will have a purple Frankenstein scar. Or a pizza-shaped scar, like mine." Judy pulled up her sleeve to show her own bumpy pizza-scar, from the time she fell chasing the ice-cream truck. Judy and Frank laughed till their appendixes hurt.

Frank helped Judy put Band-Aids all

over her patient. "Wait one week, then take the stitches out. Tell them to rest and eat prunes and plenty of Screamin' Mimi's ice cream. No, wait. That's for tonsils. Whatever! The end."

Everybody clapped really hard. "Good job," said Mr. Todd. "Nice details. You really thought of everything. I'd say it was a *smashing* success!"

M.D. = Medical Disaster

The very next day after Operation Zucchini, Frank Pearl brought a cardboard person to school. A cardboard person that looked exactly like him.

"Awesome," said Rocky. "You have a twin!"

"He's my clone. I'm Frank. He's Stein. Get it? We're Frank-and-Stein!"

Judy hoped Frank-and-Stein was not better than Operation Zucchini.

Frank Pearl told the class how you get DNA from a bone or a hair. "One cell has all your genes. You can make another one of you, exactly like you, by cloning. You can't see your genes," said Frank. "But it's all there."

"I can see my jeans. I'm wearing them," said Bradley.

"Not blue jeans. G-E-N-E, genes. DNA is the stuff that makes you YOU."

"Cool beans," said Judy.

"Scientists cloned a sheep and named her Dolly. And they cloned a bunch of mice. And some pigs, right here in Virginia," Frank told the class.

"Is that true, Mr. Todd?" asked Jessica Finch.

"It's science fiction," said Alison S.

"Like *Jurassic Park*," said Rocky.

"It's true," said Mr. Todd.

"They found a mammoth frozen in ice and they might try to clone it with DNA so mammoths won't be extinct anymore. No lie," said Frank.

"Thank you, Frank," said Mr. Todd. "Very interesting. Most of us just think of cloning as science fiction."

The rest of the morning, Frank Pearl did not pay attention once. Judy wrote him a note, but he didn't write back. She told him a joke, but he didn't laugh.

"Frank! What's wrong?" Judy asked.

"My project wasn't good."

"Was so!" said Judy. "You're a gene-ius."

"My project was cardboard. *Dead* cardboard. Nobody even believes it's real. Yours had something real. Something alive." He just stared at Peanut, the dwarf guinea pig.

"Why are you staring at Peanut?" asked Judy.

"I was just thinking how she must be lonely all by herself," said Frank.

"Judy, Frank, are you with us?" asked Mr. Todd.

"Sorry, Mr. Todd," said Judy. "Frank's worried about Peanut. Do guinea pigs get lonely? For friends?"

"Yes, well, guinea pigs do enjoy company."

"I have guinea pigs, and my guinea pig

book says you're never supposed to have just one guinea pig," said Jessica Finch.

"That's why we take turns playing with her every day," said Mr. Todd. "And we made her a fun box, remember? Now let's keep our minds on our work, okay?"

⊚   ⊚   ⊚

At morning recess, Frank found Judy and Rocky at the water fountain. "You guys have to help me get in trouble," said Frank.

"Are you crazy?" asked Rocky.

"Do you *want* to go to Antarctica?" Judy asked Frank.

"No, I just want Mr. Todd to make me stay inside for lunch recess. I need to try a science experiment. A real one. About cloning."

"Cool beans," said Rocky.

"Cool genes," said Judy, cracking herself up. "What kind of experiment?"

"Cloning Peanut. I'll make another guinea pig exactly like her. Right here in Class 3T. So she'll have a friend. Or *friends*. Real ones, not cardboard. If it works, nobody will think cloning is just science fiction."

"Cloning just works on aliens," said Rocky.

"And bones. And frozen stuff," Judy said.

"Nah-uh," said Frank.

"Well, it's against the law to practice science on animals. Stink told me. You have to use a zucchini or something."

"Everybody clones vegetables. And does experiments on *zucchinis.*"

"What's wrong with that? Real doctors practice stitches on zucchinis. It's way scientific."

"Cloning a guinea pig is way MORE scientific."

"Get real!" said Judy. "You can't just be a cloner. You need equipment. Fancy stuff, like scientists have. In labs."

"It's easy. All I need is DNA (a few hairs from Peanut), a petri dish like Rocky used for Lego germs, and electricity. Plus a little help from you guys."

"DNA means *Do Not Ask* me to experiment on animals!" said Judy. "I'll watch, but only to make sure you don't hurt Peanut."

"Let's ask Mr. Todd if we can stay inside at recess and clean Peanut's cage," said Frank. "Then nobody gets in trouble."

"Perfect," said Rocky.

"Genius," said Judy.

"Scientific," said Frank, tapping a finger to his head.

๑   ๑   ๑

When the lunch recess bell rang, Judy, Rocky, and Frank stayed inside. They lined the bottom of Peanut's cage with clean newspaper and straw. They filled up her water bottle. They gave her a new, never-been-chewed toilet-paper tube to hide in.

As soon as Mr. Todd left to get his lunch, Frank said, "Quick!" He got Mr. Todd's pointy scissors. Rocky held Peanut while Frank went *snip, snip, snip.*

"Be careful," said Judy. "I'm watching."

"Haircuts don't hurt!" said Frank. He carefully placed four hairs in the petri dish. "All we need now is electricity."

"How about the microwave?" said Rocky. Frank put the guinea pig hairs in the microwave. "Three minutes," said Frank, pressing the buttons.

"I'll say some magic words," said Rocky. "Let me think. How's this:

"Snip of hair, electric power.
How many guinea pigs per hour?
Eeny-meeny, dead Houdini.
Two, ten, twelve, fourteeny."

Ding! Frank took out the petri dish and put it back in Peanut's cage.

"Hide it under some straw," said Rocky.

"Now what do we do?" asked Judy.

"Wait," said Frank.

"This will never work," said Judy. "You should have practiced on a zucchini."

❧   ❧   ❧

The next morning, when Judy got to school, Frank was looking in Peanut's cage. Nothing! No more guinea pigs. Not two. Not ten. Not fourteeny. Just Peanut, sleeping with her head on a lettuce pillow.

"It didn't work. Cloning must be harder than I thought," said Frank.

"Told you," said Judy.

"I'm not giving up," said Frank. "Everybody knows science takes time."

They waited some more. On Thursday and Friday, when Judy got to school, Frank was there, standing over Peanut's cage. Nothing. Zip. Zero-teeny.

Peanut was alone. Un-cloned. Frank Pearl was having Double Trouble.

❀   ❀   ❀

Then, on Monday morning, it happened. While Judy was doodling guinea-pig clones with her Grouchy pencil and waiting for the start-school bell to ring, somebody yelled, "Hey! Peanut has a friend!"

Judy dropped her Grouchy pencil. She rushed over to Peanut's cage. Peanut *did* have a friend. No lie! For real and absolute positive! Not one friend, but one-two-three-four friends! One clone for every hair Frank had snipped.

"SCIENCE RULES!" Frank shouted.

"What happened?"

"Where did all these guinea pigs come from?"

"I cloned Peanut!" Frank told the class. "At first it didn't work. Then *presto*! Four guinea pigs! Double-triple-quadruple Frank-and-Stein magic!"

"They're not clones! Kids can't clone stuff."

"Are they real?"

"Did Peanut have babies?"

Judy Moody blinked once, twice, three times. She could not believe her retinas, irises, or pupils. Frank Pearl had cloned Peanut the dwarf guinea pig! She saw it with her own eyeballs. Eyeballs did not lie.

"I did it! I cloned Peanut. I'm a world-famous kid scientist! The youngest person ever to clone a guinea pig!" shouted Frank.

"I helped!" said Judy. "Don't forget me, Judy Moody, First Girl Doctor. We did it together—right, Frank? We're both famous. I bet I—I mean *we*—will be in the *Guinness Book of World Records. Ripley's Believe It or Not!*"

"Or NOT!" said one-two-three voices. Three annoying, not-funny, used-to-be-friends voices.

Frank laughed so hard he made spit fly. Rocky sprayed her, too. Worst of all, Jessica Finch was laughing her *medulla* off! She jumped up and down saying, "They're mine, they're mine, they're all my guinea

pigs. Chester had babies and we played a trick on YOU, Judy Moody!"

"You fell for it," said Frank.

"You swallowed it like a pill," said Rocky.

What was she thinking? She, Judy Moody, was not First Girl Doctor, first to help clone a guinea pig. It was all a joke. A trick. A big fat bunch of cloney baloney.

"You should see your face!" said Rocky.

"We were just *cloning* around," said Frank.

"Did you really think you *cloned* a *guinea pig*?" asked Jessica.

"Of course not," said Judy. She searched under the straw and pulled out the petri dish. Still there. It now had four hairs, eight, sixteen, thirty two. . . . The only thing that had multiplied were guinea pig hairs.

"Ha, ha! Yes, you did!" said Jessica Finch.

Judy's blood pressure went up. Her temperature was rising! She, Judy Moody, felt as silly as Bozo the Clone.

"Meet Jasmine, Cindy, Coco, and Nutmeg," said Jessica. "The Spice Girls."

"The Not-Nice girls! And boys," she said, looking at Rocky and Frank. "Mr. Todd's going to be here any minute. Don't you need to go sit down or something?"

"Yes," said Frank. "To write a letter to *Ripley's Believe It or Not*. Dear Mr. Ripley: Believe it or not, we played the best-joke-ever on our friend Judy Moody."

"ROAR!" said Judy.

M.D. = Mumpty Dumpty

The next morning, Judy Moody woke up sick. Not fake sick. Not just mad-at-her-friends sick. Real and true sick. Pain-in-the-brain sick. Hot-in-the-head sick. Frog-in-the-throat sick.

Judy ran to the mirror and stuck out her tongue. It was red all right. Not just Cherry-Ames-cough-drop red. Fire-engine red! And she saw a bumpy, mumps-of-a-lump in the back of her throat—one on each side. She, Judy Moody, had grapefruit tonsils. Bowling-ball tonsils!

The lumps made her look like a hound dog. The lumps made her look like a clone of Peanut-the-dwarf-guinea-pig (with chipmunk cheeks). The lumps made her look like Mumpty Dumpty.

Dad came into her room. He felt her forehead. He looked in her Lumpty-Dumpty throat. He took her temperature.

"You're sick, all right," said Dad, peering at the thermometer. "Looks just like what Stink had. Must be tonsillitis."

Stink came into her room before leaving for school to see if she was sick for real.

"Stink!" Judy whisper-yelled. "Get out of my room!" The lumps made her sound funny.

"Get off your broom?"

"My *room*. Get out."

"How come?"

"You don't want to catch a bad case of lumps!"

Mouse jumped up onto the bottom bunk.

"How come Mouse gets to be in there and I don't?"

"Cats don't have tonsils!"

"Stink, don't get too close to Judy!" yelled Mom.

Stink was not allowed in her room! RARE!

Staying home sick was not as fun as Judy thought it would be. When Mom brought ginger ale with a crazy straw, it went up Judy's nose. When Dad brought toast with mashed bananas, Judy took one look and said, "I think somebody already ate this." And, worst of all, TV shows in the middle of the day were full of kissing.

Mom took Judy's temperature for real, with a brand-new, no-cat-hair thermometer. Human temperature: 101.9! "I called Dr. McCavity," said Mom. "This will make you feel better." She held out some medicine. Not double-yum baby aspirin that tastes like orange Lifesavers and you get to chew it. Not triple-yum cough syrup that tastes like grape Lifesavers and you get to drink it.

A pill! Not just any old pill. A big pill. A monster pill. A pill the size of Nebraska. Mom wanted her to swallow it. Not chew it. Not drink it. Swallow it. Mom wanted her to swallow Nebraska!

Judy held her throat. "I can't swallow," she said in a sickly way.

"You were swallowing ginger ale just fine," said Mom.

"Ginger ale is not Nebraska!" Judy mumbled in her bowling-ball-tonsils voice. Her words came out all mumbly-dumbly.

"Alaska?" said Mom.

"Ne-bras-ka!" said Judy.

"Just try," said Mom. "It will make you feel lots better." Judy shut her eyes. She pinched her nose, put the pill in her mouth, and gulped down a glass of water.

"That's better," said Mom. Judy stuck out her tongue. The pill was still there!

"Judy, how are you going to be a doctor if you can't take your own medicine?"

"When I'm a doctor, I'll invent a pill-swallowing machine," said Judy.

"Okay. Never mind. I'll crush it up and you can drink it."

"Wank hoo," said Judy.

Judy felt lousy. Lousier than lice. Lumpier than mumps. Germier than worms.

A day without school was longer than a month. A day without school took a year. At least she, Bozo the Clone, did not have to go to school and face her not-so-funny friends.

Still, if they made up, she could be passing notes to Rocky right now. Or telling jokes to Frank Pearl. Or making faces at Jessica Rodent-Fink Finch. But they were all at school, school, school. Learning fun, interesting, fascinating, not pain-in-the-brain stuff, like the smallest bone in your ear is an *ossicle* (not Popsicle). Or how to spell *maxilla* (a jawbone, not Godzilla).

Judy wished she could clone a friend to have right here, right now. Instead, she counted Band-Aids in her Band-Aid collection. Three hundred thirty-seven. Plus thirteen on Hedda-Get-Betta, her doctor doll. Plus a brand-new box of thirty bug Band-Aids she got from Mom this morning just for being sick!

337 + 13 + 30 = too hard to figure out when you're not at school.

She practiced her autograph, fast and messy like real doctors.

She drew cartoons on her pillowcase with markers. Frank with a mustache. Rocky with Frankenstein hair. Jessica Finch with a rodent brain. A Stink spider web.

She made a list of all her stuffed animals.

Ned Bear
Ted Bear
Fred Bear
Cornflake (not-cloned Guinea pig)
Brownie
Tookie (Toucan)
Snowflake (Loon from Minnesota)
Auggie
Doggie
Pepper (smells like pepper)

There were more, but writing them all down gave her writer's cramp on top of bowling-ball tonsils.

She took her own temperature. With the fancy thermometer that beeped. It was not normal. It was not 98.6. Judy's temperature was 188.8! Judy's temperature was

00.0! Judy's temperature was *beep-beep-beep-beep-beep*. She, Judy Moody, had the temperature of an outer-space alien!

She stared at cracks in the ceiling. The Big Dipper. A giant hot dog. A brain (without a pain in it).

She took her temperature again. *Beeeeeeep!* Still 00.0.

"Mouse, stick out your tongue," she said. She held the thermometer under Mouse's tongue. Mouse's temperature was

. . . the letter *M*. She tried again. Mouse's temperature was *ERR*. Mouse's temperature was not even numbers. Mouse's temperature was not even human. Mouse the cat was sicker than she, Dr. Judy Moody!

"Poor baby!" said Judy. She fed Mouse an ABC (*Already Been Chewed*) mashed-up banana toast strip. Mouse loved mushed bananas.

She speed-read one book of Stink's Megazoid books about evil ants from an asteroid between Mars and Jupiter that try to take over the universe.

She read two days of Rex Morgan, M.D., comics Dad saved for her. She read three chapters of a Cherry Ames, Student Nurse, mystery till her eyes felt ker-flooey.

Finally, after about a hundred years, Stink came home from school. After about a hundred more years, he came upstairs and walked right into her room.

"Stink! Worms! Worms are everywhere. You better get out of here."

"Worms?"

"Germs, Stink. Germs! Didn't you see the sign?" Judy pointed to the sign she made on the door. "*QUARANTINE!* That means *STAY AWAY!*"

"Mom said to bring you your homework. Plus I brought other stuff."

"Like what?"

"A wooden nickel from Rocky. That he got from Suzie the Magic Lady. It has a picture of a rabbit coming out of a hat."

"I'm mad at him," said Judy. "In fact, I'm smad. And I'm not going to make up for a nickel. Wooden or not."

"Here's a card from Jessica Finch, with a pretend spelling quiz. See?" The card said:

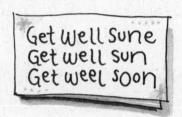

Get well Sune
Get well sun
Get weel soon

"And you have to look inside for the right answer." Judy opened the card.

It said:

None of the above!
Get well soon!
Your pal, Jessica
Finch

"I think she meant to put *Your Un-pal, Jessica Finch.*"

"And—da-da da-DA!—a love note from Frank Pearl," Stink told her.

"Give me that," said Judy.

"I made you something at school today, too." Stink took a mashed-up wad of paper out of his backpack.

"A mashed-up wad of paper?" said Judy. "Sank woo very much."

"N-O! It's a cootie catcher! I can catch germs with it. See?" Stink jumped up and down, grabbing at air.

"Stink!" said Judy. "Don't make me waff."

"Okay, okay. I won't make you waff. But look. It tells fortunes." Stink held out the cootie catcher. "Pick a number."

Judy looked at the cootie catcher. She could not find a number. All she could find were funny-looking words. "It's French!"

said Stink. "We learned French colors and numbers today. Pick one."

Judy pointed to *quatre*.

"Four," said Stink. "*Un, deux, trois, quatre.* Now pick a color."

"If you say so," said Judy. She pointed to *bleu*. It looked like *blue* with the letters mixed up.

"Blue. B-L-E-U," said Stink.

"Pick one more color." Judy pointed to another one.

"Red. R-O-U-G-E," said Stink. He lifted up the flap.

"Here's your fortune," said Stink. "*Il y a un dragon dans mon lit.*"

"What's that mean?" asked Judy. "Your friends are a bunch of cloney baloneys?"

"It means, There's a dragon in my bed," Stink told her.

"That's it? That's my fortune?"

"It's that or *My horse is dizzy*," said Stink. "Those are the only two sentences I learned so far."

"I know one more," said Judy.

"You know French?" asked Stink.

"*Oui*," said Judy. She took out her doctor pad. She wrote a prescription for Stink.

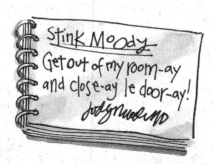

Stink Moody
Get out of my room-ay
and close-ay le door-ay!
Judy Moody MD

M.D. = Most Definitely

She, Judy Moody, was in a mood. A sick-of-being-sick mood. Even her bowling-ball pajamas didn't cheer her up. They made her think of tonsils. Judy put on her around-the-world postcard pajamas.

Dr. McCavity told Mom that Judy might not feel like herself again for about twelve days.

Twelve days! Her human temperature was rising just thinking about it! Her blood pressure was skyrocketing! Twelve days before she could stop talking like a cat under water. Twelve days before she could learn any new bones or spell *scapula* or stay away from Antarctica.

Twelve more days to feel like Bozo the Clone.

Judy made up a song. "The Twelve Days of Tonsils."

On the first day of tonsils
My brother gave to me
one cootie catcher
And a love note from Frank P.

That's as far as she got before falling asleep. Again. She slept all through the second day of tonsils.

Tonsils, Day 3: Judy drew an x-ray of her

My hand ↰

Mouse

JAWS ↘

↳

Ned Bear →

Map of my brain

hand; an x-ray of Mouse; an x-ray of Jaws, her Venus flytrap; and one of Ned Bear.

Tonsils, Day 4: Back to Dr. McCavity.

Tonsils, Day 5: BOR-ing! Judy drew a map of her brain.

Tonsils, Day 6: When she became a doctor, she would find a cure for fire-engine tonsils so sick people did not have to make x-rays of cats and maps of their brains all day.

Tonsils, Day 7: *Ding, dong!* Maybe Stink was home from school. Judy crawled back under the covers, put her head under all her stuffed animals, and pretended to be asleep.

"Knock-knock," said Stink.

"I'm asleep," said Judy.

"Knock-knock," said Stink again.

"Stink, have you been eating the BRAT diet again?"

"Just say *Who's there,*" said Stink.

"Who's there?" asked Judy.

"US!" said Rocky, Frank, and Jessica Finch. All three of her UN-best friends!

"What are YOU guys doing here?" Judy grumped. "You came to laugh at my chipmunk cheeks, didn't you? You heard I have bowling-ball tonsils and came to tell me I look like Mumpty Dumpty."

"No!" said Frank. "We —"

"Wait. Let me guess. You cloned an anteater. An armadillo. An aardwolf. Ha, ha. Very funny."

"We brought you something to make

up . . . I mean, we brought you something to make you feel better," said Rocky.

"Nothing will make me feel better," said Judy. "I feel lousy. As in licey. As in not-nicey."

"But this really works," said Frank.

"Is it a pill?" asked Judy. "I hope it's not a pill the size of Nebraska."

"No."

"Is it a prune? I hope it's not a goony old prune."

"Nope."

"Is it a Band-Aid? I hope it *is* a Band-Aid with words."

"No, no, and nope," said Jessica Finch.

"Does it squeak? I hear squeaking!"

"Yes!" said Jessica.

"Does it have fur, fins, or fangs?"

"Yes!" said Stink.

Rocky held up a shirt with words.

"A shirt does not have fur or fins or fangs."

"Look," said Frank, turning the shirt over. "We made it for you at Rocky's house." The shirt said PAWS FOR HEALING. It had blue guinea-pig paw prints all over it.

"Hello! A shirt doesn't squeak!" said Judy.

"No," said Rocky. "But pets do. We brought you animals to pet!"

"Just like Paws for Healing," said Frank.

"So you can lower your blood pressure and not feel sick," said Jessica.

Rocky had brought Houdini, his pet iguana. Frank had brought a red-and-purple fish in a jar, and Jessica Finch had brought Chester and all four of the baby guinea pigs—the (un-cloned) Spice Girls!

Stink went to his room and brought back Toady.

"You brought half the zoo!" said Judy.

"And I got you a real Paws for Healing button," said Stink. "From the hospital gift shop." He held out a button that said I'M IN CHARGE OF CRITTER-COOL CARE.

"Cool!" said Frank.

"Critter-cool!" said Judy. She put the Paws for Healing shirt on over her around-the-world postcard pajamas. She pinned the button to her shirt.

Rocky held out Houdini. "You hold him, while I clip his toenails."

Snip, snip, snip.

"He has more toenails than Stink!" Judy laughed.

Frank set his fish on Judy's desk, next to her jelly bean collection. "My aunt got me this Siamese fighting fish when I was sick. I named her Judy."

"Same-same!" said Judy.

"You can keep her till you get better. I know you can't pet her, but it's supposed to relax you and make you feel better just to watch her."

"I promise I'll watch her all the time," said Judy.

"Look! Judy the Fighting Fish is blowing bubbles!" said Stink.

"Rare!" said the not-fish Judy.

"And you can play with Toady anytime you want," said Stink. "As long as you don't operate on him."

"I won't," said Judy. "I promise."

Jessica brought special shampoo, and they each gave a guinea pig a bath. "Coco hates baths," said Jessica. "But guinea pigs have to be clean."

"Just like doctors!" Judy said.

When they were done, they each got to blow-dry their guinea pigs.

"Nutmeg's ready for a party!" said Judy, stroking the guinea pig's fur. Jessica got Cindy to roll over twice, and Coco twitched her whiskers at Cornflake, Judy's stuffed guinea pig.

"That means hello in guinea pig," said Jessica. "She's trying to make friends!" Everybody cracked up.

Nutmeg squirmed out of Judy's arms and ran in circles around her room.

"Uh-oh!" said Jessica. Nutmeg ran around Judy's floor pillow. She ran around Ned Bear, Ted Bear, and Fred Bear, the trash can, and Judy's doctor kit. She ran around and around Judy's squiggle rug.

"Catch her!" said Stink.

Everybody chased Nutmeg. Even Mouse. Nutmeg hid under Judy's squiggle rug. Jessica caught her with an ice-cream container.

"Phew! That was a close one, girl," said

Judy, rubbing the guinea pig's tummy. "Hey, look! Nutmeg likes tummy rubs!"

"She likes you," said Jessica.

"Aw. I wish I could keep her forever and ever," said Judy. "I promise not to clone her."

"She's still too young," said Jessica. "But when the Spice Girls get older, my dad says we can take them to the hospital for Paws for Healing. You know, help some more kids feel better."

"RARE!" said Judy.

When everybody had gone home, Judy climbed back under the covers and leaned against all her stuffed animals. She was feeling not-so-sick-anymore. Her tonsils did not feel so lumpy. She, Judy Moody, did not feel so grumpy. Friends were better than prunes. Friends were better than medicine. Friends were better than all the ginger ale, ABC toast, and TV in the world.

Her temperature was dropping. So was her blood pressure. Her tonsils were shrinking fast. Most definitely!

Judy Moody took out her mood journal. She wrote herself a poem. A moody poem. A Mumpty Dumpty poem.

Mumpty Dumpty had a great case of lumps.
Mumpty Dumpty had a worse case of grumps.
All Judy's brothers and all Judy's friends
Helped put Mumpty back together again.

Judy took out her doctor pad. She, Dr. Judy Moody, wrote *herself* a prescription.

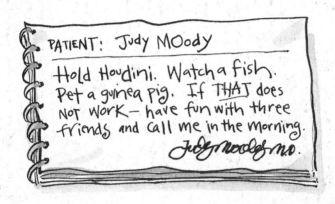

PATIENT: Judy MOody

Hold Houdini. Watch a fish.
Pet a guinea pig. If THAT does
NOT work — have fun with three
friends and call me in the morning.
Judy Moody M.D.

Last but not least, Judy signed her name with a scribbly doctor autograph.

Megan McDonald

is the award-winning author of the Judy Moody series. She says that most of Judy's stories "grew out of anecdotes about growing up with my four sisters." She confesses, "I *am* Judy Moody. Same-same! In my family of sisters, we're famous for exaggeration. Judy Moody is me . . . exaggerated." Megan McDonald lives with her husband in northern California.

Peter H. Reynolds

says he felt an immediate connection to Judy Moody because, "having a daughter, I have witnessed firsthand the adventures of a very independent-minded girl." Peter H. Reynolds lives in Massachusetts, just down the street from his twin brother.

Praise for
Judy Moody, M.D.

A *Disney Adventures* Magazine
Book Award Winner

"Proves laughter can be contagious." —*Booklist*

"As always, there are facts to be learned and loads of
puns and playful language to entertain readers. This
is another winner, 'for real and absolute positive.'"
—*School Library Journal*

Be sure to read Judy's next adventure

DOUBLE RARE!

Judy Moody has her own website!

Come visit **www.judymoody.com**
for the latest in all things Judy Moody, including:

- ◉ All you need to know about the best-ever
  Judy Moody Fan Club

- ◉ Answers to all your V.I.Q.s (very important
  questions) about Judy

- ◉ Way-not-boring stuff about Megan McDonald
  and Peter H. Reynolds

- ◉ Double-cool activities that will be sure to put you
  in a mood—and not a bad mood, a good mood!

- ◉ Totally awesome T.P. Club info!

Look out, Judy Moody!

Stink
is starring in
his very own series!

Here's a sneak peek at Stink's first adventure. . . .

When Stink woke up the next morning, his bed felt as big as a country. The ceiling was up there with the sky. And it was a long way down to the floor.

When he went to brush his teeth, even the sink seemed too tall.

"Yipe! I really am shrinking," said Stink, checking himself out in the mirror. Were his arms a little shorter? Was his head a little smaller?

Stink got dressed. He put on up-

and-down-striped pants and an up-and-down-striped shirt.

"What's with the stripes?" asked Judy.

"Makes me look taller," said Stink.

"If you say so," said Judy.

"What?"

"If you really want to look taller, here's what you do." Judy handed him a fancy shampoo-type bottle. "Put this hair gel on your hair and leave it in for ten minutes. Then you'll be able to comb your hair so it sticks straight up. Sticking-up hair will make you look taller."

An excerpt from *Stink: The Incredible Shrinking Kid*

Stink put the goopy goop in his hair. He left it in his hair while he made his bed. He left it in his hair while he packed up his backpack. He left it in his hair all through breakfast.

"We could play baseball, and you could be *short*stop," Judy told him.

"So funny I forgot to laugh," said Stink.

Judy pointed to Stink's hair. "Hey, I think it's working!" she said.

"Really? Do you think people will notice?"

"They'll notice," said Judy.

Stink ran upstairs to look in the

mirror. "HEY! My HAIR! It's ORANGE!"

"Don't worry," said Judy. "It'll wash out . . . in about a week."

"I look like a carrot!" said Stink.

"Carrots are tall," said Judy, and she laughed all the way to the bus stop.

✶ ✶ ✶

Stink's friend Elizabeth sat next to him in class. They were the shortest kids in Class 2D, so they sat up front. "Hi, Elizabeth," said Stink.

"I'm not Elizabeth anymore," she told Stink. "From now on, call me Sophie of the Elves."

An excerpt from *Stink: The Incredible Shrinking Kid*

"Okay. I have a new name, too. The Incredible Shrinking Stink."

"But, Stink, you look taller today," said Elizabeth.

"It's just the hair," said Stink. "I'm still short."

"Not to an elf. To an elf, you'd be a giant. To an elf, you would be the Elf King."

"Thanks, Sophie of the Elves," said Stink.

The bell rang, and Mrs. Dempster passed out spelling words. Three of the new words were *shrink, shrank, shrunk.* At lunch, the dessert was strawberry *short*cake. And in

Reading, Mrs. Dempster read everybody a book called *The Shrinking of Treehorn.*

The book was all about a boy who plays games and reads cereal boxes and gets shorter and shorter. He keeps shrinking and shrinking. Then, just when he becomes a normal size again, he turns green!

"Any comments?" Mrs. Dempster asked when the story was over.

Stink raised his hand. "Is that a true story?"

Mrs. D. laughed. "I'm afraid not," she said. "It's fantasy."

"Fantasy's my favorite!" said

Sophie of the Elves. "Especially hobbits and elves."

"Are you sure it's fantasy?" asked Stink. "Because that kid is a lot like me. Because I'm . . . I'm . . ." Stink could not make himself say *shrinking.*

"Because you both turned another color?" asked Webster.

"Um, because I like to read everything on the cereal box, too," said Stink.

"Okay," said Mrs. Dempster. "Let's see. Who's going to carry the milk from the cafeteria today?" Stink was barely paying attention.

He never got asked to carry the milk.

"How about Mr. James Moody?" asked Mrs. Dempster.

"Me?" asked Stink. He sat up taller. "I get to carry the milk?"

Stink walked down the second-grade hallway. It looked longer than usual. And wider. He took the stairs down to the cafeteria. Were there always this many stairs? His legs felt shorter. Like they shrink, shrank, shrunk.

Be sure to check out
Stink's adventures!

Experience
all of
Judy Moody's
moods!

Judy Moody
Declares Independence

Alia Irizarry
Ortiz

Books by Megan McDonald and Peter H. Reynolds:

#1 – *Judy Moody*

#2 – *Judy Moody Gets Famous!*

#3 – *Judy Moody Saves the World!*

#4 – *Judy Moody Predicts the Future*

#5 – *Judy Moody, M.D.: The Doctor Is In!*

#6 – *Judy Moody Declares Independence*

#7 – *Judy Moody Around the World in 8½ Days*

#1 – *Stink: The Incredible Shrinking Kid*

#2 – *Stink and the Incredible Super-Galactic Jawbreaker*

#3 – *Stink and the World's Worst Super-Stinky Sneakers*

The Judy Moody Mood Journal

Judy Moody's Double-Rare Way-Not-Boring Book of Fun Stuff to Do

Books by Megan McDonald:

Ant and Honey Bee: What a Pair!

The Sisters Club

Books by Peter H. Reynolds:

The Dot

Ish

So Few of Me

Judy Moody
Declares Independence

HUZZAH!

Megan McDonald

illustrated by
Peter H. Reynolds

CANDLEWICK PRESS
CAMBRIDGE, MASSACHUSETTS

First paperback edition 2007

The Library of Congress has cataloged the hardcover edition as follows:

McDonald, Megan.
Judy Moody declares independence / by Megan McDonald ; illustrated by
Peter H. Reynolds. — 1st ed.
p. cm.
Summary: After learning about the American Revolution on a family trip to
Boston, Massachusetts, Judy Moody makes her own Declaration of
Independence and tries to prove that she is responsible enough to have more
freedoms, such as a higher allowance and her own bathroom.
ISBN 978-0-7636-2361-6 (hardcover)
[1. Responsibility—Fiction. 2. Boston (Mass.)—Fiction. 3. Humorous stories.]
I. Reynolds, Peter, date, ill. II. Title.
PZ7.M1487Jn 2005
[Fic]—dc22   2004051833

ISBN 978-0-7636-2800-0 (paperback)

2 4 6 8 10 9 7 5 3 1

Printed in the United States of America

This book was typeset in Stone Informal and Judy Moody.
The illustrations were done in watercolor, tea, and ink.

Candlewick Press
2067 Massachusetts Avenue
Cambridge, Massachusetts 02140

visit us at www.candlewick.com

In memory of Jon and Mary Louise McDonald

M. M.

To Diana GaikaZova, who declared independence
and is making history of her own

P. H. R.

Table of Contents

Bean Town, MOO-sa-chu-setts.............1

Freedom (from Stink) Trail...............11

Sugar and Spies.........................21

In a Nark...............................35

The Purse of Happiness.................45

Huzzah!................................59

The UN-Freedom Trail...................68

The Boston Tub Party...................80

Sybil La-Dee-Da........................97

The Declaration of UN-Independence.....106

Yankee Doodle Dandy....................126

Judy Moody

Judy Moodington

Dad

Richard "John Hancock" Moody

Mom

Kate "Betsy Ross" Moody

John Hancock

Fancy first signer
of the Declaration of
Independence

Tori

Not a Tory; fab collector
of sugar packets

Who

Sybil Ludington

Sybil La-Dee-Da,
girl Paul Revere

Paul Revere

Bell ringer,
false teeth maker,
midnight rider

Stink

Town crier, fond
of musical toilets

Frank

← →

Partners in crime:
the Boston Tub Party

Rocky

Bean Town, MOO-sa-chu-setts

HEAR YE! HEAR YE!

She, Judy Moody, was in Boston! Bean Town! As in Mas-sa-chu-setts. As in the Cradle of Liberty, Birthplace of Ben Famous Franklin and Paul Revere. Land of the Boston Tea Party and the Declaration of Independence.

"Boston rules," said Judy.

Three best things about Boston so far were:

1. Freedom from two whole days of school (including one spelling test, two nights of homework, and a three-page book report)
2. Freedom from riding in the car next to Stink for ten million hours
3. Freedom from brushing hair every day

She, Judy Moody, Rider of the First Subway in America, was finally on her way to the real-and-actual Freedom Trail! The place where her country started. Where it all began.

The American Revolution! The Declaration of Independence! Freedom!

R A R E!

Judy and her family climbed up the stairs and out into the fresh air, heading for the information booth on Boston Common, where Dad bought a guide to the Freedom Trail.

"Did you know there used to be cows right here in this park?" asked Stink. "It says so on that sign."

"Welcome to MOO-sa-chu-setts!" announced Judy. She cracked herself up. If Rocky or Frank Pearl were here, they'd crack up, too.

"Just think," Judy told Stink. "Right now, this very minute, while I am about to follow in the footsteps of freedom, Mr. Todd is probably giving Class 3T a spelling test

back in Virginia. Nineteen number-two pencil erasers are being chewed right this very second."

"You're lucky. I had to miss Backwards Shirt Day today."

"The trail starts right here at Boston Common," Dad said.

"Can we go look at ducks?" asked Stink. "Or frogs? On the map there's a frog pond."

"Stink, we're going on the *Freedom* Trail. Not the *Frog* Trail."

"What should we do first?" asked Mom.

"Tea Party! Boston Tea Party Ship!" said Judy, jumping up and down.

"We came all the way to Boston for a *tea party*?" asked Stink.

"Not that kind of tea party," Mom said.

"The people here first came over from England," said Dad, "because they wanted to have freedom from the king telling them what to do."

"Dad, is this another LBS? Long Boring Story?" asked Stink.

"It's way NOT boring, Stink," said Judy. "It's the beginning of our whole country. This wouldn't even be America if it weren't for this giant tea party they had. See, the Americans wouldn't drink tea from over there in England. No way."

"Not just tea," said Mom. "The British made them pay unfair taxes on lots of things, like paper and sugar. They called it the Stamp Act and the Sugar Act. But the

Americans didn't have any say about what all the tax money would be used for."

"I don't get it," said Stink.

"We didn't want some grumpy old king to be boss of us," said Judy.

"America wanted to be grown-up and independent," said Mom. "Free from England. Free to make up its own rules and laws."

"So Thomas Jefferson wrote the Declaration of Independence," said Dad.

"And a lot of important people signed it real fancy," said Judy, "like John Hancock, First Signer of the Declaration. Right, Mom?"

"Right," said Mom.

"Before we hit the Freedom Trail, let's go

see the Liberty Tree," said Dad. "That's where people stood to make important speeches about freedom."

"Like a town crier?" asked Judy.

"That's right," said Dad. "Here we are."

"I don't see any tree," said Stink. "All I see is some old sign on some old building."

"The British cut it down," Dad said. "But that didn't stop the Americans. They just called it the Liberty Stump and kept right on making speeches."

"I don't see any tree stump," said Stink.

"Hello! Use your imagination, Stink," said Judy.

"Kids, stand together in front of the sign so Dad can take your picture."

"I still don't see what's so big about the American Revolution," mumbled Stink.

"Some of us like the American Revolution, Stink," said Judy. "Let freedom ring!" she shouted. Hair flew across her face.

"Judy, I thought I asked you to use a brush this morning," Mom said.

"I did use it," said Judy. "On that pink fuzzy pillow in our hotel room!" Mom poked at Judy's hair, trying to smooth out the bumps. Judy squeezed her eyes shut, making an Ouch Face. Dad snapped the picture.

"Hear ye! Hear ye!" called Judy. "I, Judy Moody, hereby declare freedom from brushing my hair!"

"Then I declare it from brushing my teeth!" said Stink.

"P.U." said Judy, squinching up her nose.

Dad snapped another picture.

Three worst things about Boston so far were:

1. *Stink*
2. *Stink*
3. *Stink*

The Freedom (from Stink) Trail

"Time to hit the Freedom Trail!" said Dad.

"Let's head up Park Street," Mom said, pointing to a line of red bricks in the sidewalk. "Follow the red brick road!"

"Look!" Judy cried, running up the hill. "Look at that big fancy gold dome!"

"That's the State House," said Mom. "Where the governor works."

"Judy!" Dad called. "No running ahead. Stick close to us."

"Aw," said Judy. "No fair. This is supposed to be the *Freedom* Trail."

"Stay where Dad and I can keep an eye on you," said Mom.

"Roar!" said Judy.

After the State House, Mom and Dad led them to Park Street Church, where the song "My Country 'Tis of Thee" was sung for the very first time.

Stink looked for famous-people initials carved into a tree outside. PLOP! Something hit Stink on the head. "YEE-UCK! Bird poo!" said Stink. Judy cracked up. Mom wiped it off with a tissue.

Stink sang:

> *"My country pooed on me*
>
> *Right near the Pigeon Tree.*
>
> *Of thee I sing. . . ."*

"Mom! Dad!" said Judy, covering her ears. "Make him stop!"

Judy ran ahead. "Hurry up, you guys! The church has an old graveyard!"

Mom read the plaque at the entrance: "'May the youth of today . . . be inspired with the patriotism of Paul Revere.'"

"Paul Revere's grave is here!" Judy shouted. "So is John Hancock's, First Signer of the Declaration. For real!"

Judy saw gravestones with angel wings, skulls and bones, and a giant hand with one finger pointing to the sky.

"'Here lies buried Samuel Adams, Signer of the Declaration of Independence,'" Dad read. "Did you know he also gave the secret signal at the Boston Tea Party?"

"'Here lyes y body of Mary Goose,'" Stink read. "Boy, they sure did spell funny."

"And I thought I was the world's worst speller," said Judy. She took out pencil and paper from her backpack and made a sketch of Mother Goose's grave. Stink made drawings of a skull and bones, a leaf, and a sidewalk crack.

"Do we have to keep seeing stuff?" Stink asked when they got to the Ben Franklin statue. "So far it's just a bunch of dead guys and some old stuff that isn't even there anymore."

"But what about the Boston Tea Party?" asked Judy.

"AW!" Stink whined. "I have to go to the bathroom."

"Stink, don't be the town crier," said Judy. "I mean, the town *crybaby*!"

"Tell you what," said Mom. "Dad, why don't you and Judy go see the Paul Revere House. I'll take Stink to the bathroom, and we'll meet back here."

"Great idea!" said Dad.

Judy and Dad walked and walked. At last they came to 19 North Square. "Did you know that Paul Revere made false teeth?" Dad asked. "And he made the first bells in America. He even drew cartoons."

"Wow!" said Judy. "All that on top of riding his horse lightning-fast and warning everybody that the British were coming!"

"That's right," Dad said. "A friend of Paul Revere's climbed out a window and over a rooftop to give the lantern signal from the Old North Church: one if by land, two if by sea . . . "

"Star-spangled bananas!" said Judy.

"And it says here he rode all the way to Philadelphia to tell them the news about the Boston Tea Party," Dad said.

"Tea party? Did somebody say *tea party*?" asked Judy.

"Okay, okay. Let's head back to meet Mom and Stink."

Judy ran up to Stink. "You missed it, Stink!" She told him all about the guy climbing out the window and giving the secret signal.

"Who cares?" said Stink. "We saw some-thing better!"

"What?" said Judy. "A two-hundred-year-old toilet?"

"No, a *musical* toilet!" said Stink. "You put a quarter in—"

"You have to pay to go to the bath-room?" Judy asked. "That stinks."

"You go inside, and you're in this round room, and it's all white and clean—really, really clean—and it plays music!"

"I thought he'd never come out," Mom said.

"C'mon. We can quick hop the subway over to the Tea Party Ship," said Dad.

"Finally!" said Judy.

"More old stuff? I declare NO FAIR!" Stink shouted. The shout heard 'round the world.

Sugar and Spies

She, Judy Moody, declared independence from Stink. She ran up the planks ahead of him. She climbed aboard the *Beaver*. The Boston Tea Party Ship!

"Is this a real ship?" Stink asked.

"It's a real ship," said a guy wearing a wig and dressed like Paul Revere. "But it's not old, like the real *Beaver*. We built it to show what the Tea Party ship looked like."

"Finally! Something NOT old!" said Stink.

Judy climbed some ropes. So did Stink. She tried out a hammock. So did Stink. She went down the ladder into the dark cargo hold. So did Stink.

"Stink! How can I declare independence from you if you keep following me everywhere?"

Judy went back on deck. The Wig Guy was explaining about the guys who wore disguises, sneaked aboard ship after dark, and threw a million dollars worth of tea overboard.

"Who'd like to try throwing tea into Boston Harbor?"

Judy rushed to the front. Stink followed (of course!). They picked up bales tied with rope. Judy heaved a bale of tea over the side. "I won't drink tea! Taxes are NO FAIR!"

"Take that, King George!" said Stink as he tossed a bale off the ship.

"Who else wants to try?" Wig Guy pointed to a girl wearing bunny ears and carrying a purse that said BONJOUR BUNNY.

"C'mon, now. Wouldn't you like to give 'er the old heave-ho?"

"No," said the girl. "I quite like tea." She had a funny accent.

"From England, are you?" asked the man. The girl nodded.

"How exciting. This lass has come all the way from *across the pond*, as they say, just to see our ship!" The girl beamed.

"Glad to have you aboard, lassie!" Wig Guy shook her hand. "The Revolution was a long time ago. Let's be mates!"

The girl with the freckles and the funny voice was from England! Where they drank tea and had a queen. Judy had never met a real-live person from a whole other country before. Rare!

"I'm going to talk to her," Judy told Stink.

"You can't! She's a Redcoat! One of the Bad Guys!"

Judy looked around, but the Girl from

Across the Pond was nowhere in sight. Just then, Mom called for Judy and Stink to go to the gift shop.

Judy wandered up and down the aisles. Boxes of tea, bags of tea, tins of tea. Teapots and teacups and teaspoons. Stink followed her.

"Look! A tricorn hat!" She tried it on. "Stink, can I borrow some money? I want to get this hat."

"It's my money," said Stink. "From my allowance. Use your own."

"But I already spent mine at the Old North Church gift shop. On a Declaration of Independence and a *Paul Revere's Ride* flip book. I should get more allowance because I'm older than you. C'mon, Stink. You always have money."

"No way," said Stink.

"Redcoat!" Judy said.

"Yankee Doodle!" Stink said.

"Lobsterback!" said Judy.

"Chowder Head!" said Stink.

"Red Belly!" said Judy.

"Blue Belly!" said Stink.

"Kids! Keep it down," said Dad.

"Stink, stop following me around and stop getting me in trouble. Don't forget, I'm independent of you now." Judy walked away, past the drums and pennywhistles.

There she was! The tea drinker girl from England was not even looking at tea. She

was looking at snow globes. Of Boston. Judy liked snow globes, too!

"Are you really a Red—I mean, from England?"

"Of course," said the girl. Her voice sounded snooty, as if the queen herself made the girl's bed.

"Does the queen make your bed?" asked Judy.

"WHAT?"

"Never mind. I was just wondering. What's your name?" Judy asked.

"Victoria. But you can call me Tori."

Stink popped up from behind a spinner rack. "Tory! Tories were the Bad Guys in the Revolution!" he said.

"Stink, stop spying on us!" said Judy.

She turned back to Tori. "Um . . . what's that rabbit on your purse?" she blurted.

"It's Bonjour Bunny. I'm freaky for Bonjour Bunny! I have the backpack, jim-jams, and sleeping bag. I even have my own Bonjour Bunny alarm clock! I just got the phone for my birthday. And the flannel, I mean washcloth, for my bathroom in our flat."

"Flat? You have a tire in your house?"

"No, it's our apartment. Mum has her bathroom, and I have mine."

PHONE! BATHROOM! WASHCLOTH! Judy's mom and dad would never let her have a phone. Or her own bathroom. At home, Judy had to use any old washcloth. Even ones with Stink cooties.

"I collect stuff, too," said Judy. "Mostly Barbie-doll heads and pizza tables. My newest collection is ABC gum. I stick it on the lamp in my room."

"ABC gum?" asked the girl.

"Already Been Chewed—I label each piece, like a rock collection."

"Fab!" said Tori. "I never heard of that."

"And I collect pencils," said Judy. "And Band-Aids."

"Brilliant!" said Tori. "We call them plasters, not Band-Aids."

"Do you collect tea?" asked Judy.

"No. But I do collect sugar packets with pictures on them." Tori opened her coin purse. It was filled with sugar packets! She, Judy Moody, Collector of the World, had never even *thought* of collecting sugar packets.

"I have American presidents and flags of the world," said Tori. "Famous paintings. Hotel names . . . boring! Famous women, too. See? Here's one of Susan B. Anthony."

"Do you have Amelia Bloomer? She gave a speech on Boston Common in her undies," said Judy.

"In her knickers?" asked Tori.

"Really they were bloomers. Some people call them pant-a-loons. Because they're *loons* if they think girls can't wear pants," said Judy.

"At least it wasn't in her nuddy pants,"

Tori whispered. "That means *bare naked*!" Judy and Tori cracked up.

"I did get some at the snack bar with Ben Franklin sayings!" Tori added. "See?"

Judy read the sugar packets. "'Don't cry over spilled milk.' 'If your head is made of wax, don't stand out in the sun.'" She

cracked up some more. "Brilliant!" said Judy. "My little brother will be so jealous!" She looked around. She didn't see Stink anywhere.

"The short one? Been spying on us? Maybe he's gone to the loo."

"The what?" Judy asked.

"You know." Tori pointed to the bathroom.

"The loo! That's cuckoo!" Judy didn't see her mom and dad either. "Well, I better go find my family," she said. "We're supposed to eat lunch at the snack bar."

"Me too! I'll go and fetch my mum."

"See you there," said Judy.

"Cheers!" said Tori. "Wait—what's your name?"

"Judy. Judy Moody."

"Brilliant!" said Tori.

In a Nark

Judy found her mom, dad, and Stink in the checkout line. Dad was getting a ship-in-the-bottle kit to make a model of the *Beaver*. Mom was buying stuff to sew a cross-stitch pillow of the Paul Revere statue with the Old North Church in the background. Stink was holding a tin of Boston Harbor tea and waving a flag with a snake on it that said, DON'T TREAD ON ME.

Judy paid for her hat (with Stink's money), and they walked to the snack bar.

"You owe me four dollars and ninety-seven cents plus tax," said Stink.

"Tax! Mom! Dad! Stink's going all British on me. I need a raise in my allowance so I can pay Stink back."

"We'll talk about more allowance when we get home," said Mom.

"Time for lunch," said Dad. "I need a coffee."

"Not tea?" asked Mom.

"Just being loyal to my country," Dad said.

"Can I try coffee?" asked Judy. "I want to be loyal to my country, too."

"Dream on," said Dad.

"How about tea?"

"How about chocolate milk," said Dad.

"The Boston Chocolate Milk Party. How UN-Revolutionary."

Judy ordered a Ben Franklin (grilled cheese with French fries). In the middle of bite three of her Ben Franklin, she said, "Hey, there's Tori!"

"Tori the Tory," said Stink.

Tori and her mom came over. While everybody met, Tori showed Judy all the new Bonjour Bunny stuff in her bag.

"You have all the luck!" said Judy. "I need more allowance. For sure and absolute positive."

"Mum gives me two pounds a week," said Tori.

"Star-spangled bananas!" said Judy. Tori got *pounds* of allowance! All Judy got was a few stinky ounces.

"C'mon," said Tori. "Let's collect more Ben Franklin sugar packets." While the grownups talked and Stink blew bubbles in his un-Revolutionary chocolate milk, Judy and Tori sat at an empty table and spread out all the sugar packets.

A penny saved is a penny earned.

Don't cry over spilled milk.

Fish and visitors stink after three days.

"Let's make up our own!" said Judy. She wrote on the backs of the packets:

A penny saved is never as much as Stink has.
Fish and little brothers stink after three days.

"Crikey! That's jolly good!" said Tori. She made one up, too:

Don't cry over spilled chocolate milk.

Judy taught Tori how to play Concentration with sugar packets. Tori showed Judy how to build a sugar-packet castle. When it came time to go, Judy did not want to leave her new friend.

"Mom? Dad? Can Tori come back to the hotel with us?" Judy asked.

"Or can Judy go swimming at our hotel with us?" Tori asked her mom.

"Can Tori come to Chinatown with us tonight?"

"Can Judy sleep over at our hotel? We

can sleep on the floor like we do in our flat at home."

Mom looked at Dad. Dad looked at Mom. "I don't think so, honey."

"AW! Why not?" asked Judy.

"We've only just met Tori," said Mom.

"Yes, that's right, girls," said Tori's mom.

"Please, Mum," said Tori. "Judy's ever so fun."

"Judy and her family have got their own plans," said Tori's mom. "And we have tickets for the Duck Tour later this afternoon."

"Besides, we have to get an early start in the morning, Judy. It's back home to Virginia tomorrow," Dad said.

"Please-please-pretty-please with sugar packets on top?" Judy begged. "This is our one and only chance. We might never see each other again ever. Please? It would be brilliant!"

Mom shook her head no.

"Not even on account of the Revolution? I'm American and she's British and it's really good if we're friends. We could change history!"

"We said no, honey," Dad said.

"Well," said Tori's mom, "it's been lovely meeting you and your family, Judy. Hasn't it, Tori?"

"Crumb cakes!" said Tori. She hung her head. She kicked at a stone.

"Now, don't get in a nark," said Tori's mom.

"Who's going in an ark?" asked Stink.

"A nark," said Tori's mom. "It means a bad mood."

"Ohh. My sister has narks ALL the time," said Stink.

"Maybe when Tori gets back to London and we get home," said Mom, "you two can write to each other. Like pen pals!"

"That would be lovely," said Tori's mom. "Wouldn't it, Tori?" Tori didn't answer. "Well, we'd better nip off," said her mother.

"Here, you can have these," Tori told Judy. "To remember me by." She gave Judy her Bonjour Bunny ears.

Judy gave Tori a whole pack of gum. "You can start your own ABC collection," said Judy.

Tori wrote down her address in London. Judy gave Tori her address in Virginia. "We can send each other sugar packets!" Tori whispered. "It'll be the bee's knees!"

Judy did not feel like the bee's knees.

She, Judy Moody, was in a nark. Not a good nark. A bad nark.

The Purse of Happiness

Judy was in a nark for four hundred forty-four miles. She was in a nark all the way through Rhode Island, Connecticut, New York, and Pennsylvania. (She slept through Maryland.) She was even in a nark through Home of the Presidents, Washington, D.C.

Judy Moody was in a nark for seven hours and nineteen minutes. A Give-Me-Liberty nark.

"Mom! Judy won't play car games with me."

Stink wanted to count cows. Stink wanted to play the license plate game. Stink wanted to play Scrabble Junior.

"Judy," said Mom. "Play Scrabble with your brother."

"It's *baby* Scrabble!" said Judy. "I know. Let's play the silent game. Where you see how long you can go without talking."

"Hardee-har-har," said Stink.

"I win!" said Judy.

"Hey, you two," said Mom.

"It's her fault," said Stink.

"Judy, you're not still in a mood about Tori, are you?" asked Mom.

"You never let me do stuff," said Judy. "You should hear all the stuff Tori gets to do in England! She has tons of sleepovers. She even has her own phone. And her own bathroom! And she gets pounds of allowance. You think I'm still a baby or something."

"Or something," said Stink.

"Judy, if you want us to treat you like you're more grown-up, and if you want a raise in your allowance, then you'll have to show us that you can be more responsible."

"And not always get in a mood about everything," said Dad.

"I've never even had a sleepover before!" said Judy.

"Maybe when we get home, you can have a sleepover with Jessica Finch," said Mom.

"When cows read," said Judy. She, Judy Moody, was moving to England. She chewed two pieces of ABC gum, loud as a cow. She blew bubbles. *Pop! Pop! Pop-pop-pop!*

"She's still in a mood!" announced Stink.

In her mood journal, Judy made up nicknames for Stink all the rest of the way home.

Stinker
Stink-o-lator
Stink-o-rama
The Stinkster

Stink Bug
The Stink Man
Stink McFink
Stink-a-roni

☙ ☙ ☙

When Judy got home, she dragged her tote bag upstairs to her room. *Thwump, thwump, thwump.* She dragged her backpack, her blanket, her pillow, and her sock monkey. And her stuff from the gift shop. She shut the door and climbed up into her secret hideaway (her top bunk).

She, Judy Moody, was supposed to be writing her makeup book report, as in not waiting till the very, very last minute. Instead, she declared freedom from home-work.

Then she, Judy Moody, had an idea. A freedom idea. A John Hancock idea. A Declaration of Independence idea.

She did not even stop to call Rocky and tell him about the Boston Tea Party Ship and the Giant Milk Bottle that sold star-spangled bananas. She did not even stop to call Frank and tell him about Mother Goose's grave and the musical toilet.

That could wait till tomorrow.

But some things could not wait.

Judy gazed in awe at the copy of the Declaration of Independence she'd gotten in Boston. It was on old-timey brown paper with burned edges that looked like tea had been spilled on it. Judy squinted to try to read the fancy-schmancy handwriting.

When in the bones of human events . . . blah blah blah . . . we hold these truths . . . more blah blah . . . alien rights . . . Life, Liberty, and the Purse of Happiness.

She, Judy Moody, would hereby, this day, make the Judy Moody Declaration of

Independence. With alien rights and her own Purse of Happiness and everything.

Judy pulled out the paper place mat she had saved from the Milk Street Cafe. The back was brown from chocolate-milk spills. Perfect! At last, Judy Moody knew what Ben Franklin meant when he said *Don't cry over spilled milk.*

The real Declaration of Independence was written with a quill pen. Luckily, she, Judy Moody, just happened to have a genuine-and-for-real quill pen from the gift shop.

Look out, world! Judy mixed some water into the black powder that came with the pen, dipped the feather pen into the ink, and wrote:

Judy Moody's
Declaration of Independence
(WITH 7 ALIEN RIGHTS)

I, Judy Moody, hereby declare...

- Freedom from brushing my hair
- Freedom from little brothers (as in STINK)
- Freedom from baby bedtime (stay up later than Stink)
- Freedom from homework
- Freedom to have sleepovers
- Freedom to have my own bathroom (and washcloth!)
- Freedom to get pounds of allowance

Judy Moody

She signed it in cursive with fancy squiggles, just like Mr. Revolution Himself, First Signer of the Declaration, John Hancock. And she made it big so Dad could see it without his reading glasses, just like they did for King George.

Judy ran downstairs wearing her tricorn hat. Where was Mouse? Judy found her curled up in the dirty-laundry pile. She jingled her cat like a bell. "Hear ye! Hear ye!" she called. Mom, Dad, and Stink came into the family room.

"I will now hereby read my very own Judy Moody Declaration of Independence, made hereby on this day, the 4th of Judy. I hereby stand up for these alien rights—

stuff like Life, Liberty, and definitely the Purse of Happiness." Judy cleared her throat. "Did I say *hereby*?"

"Only ten hundred times," said Stink.

Judy read the list aloud, just like a town crier (not town crybaby). At the end, she took off her tricorn hat and said, "Give me liberty or give me death!"

"Very funny," said Dad.

"Very clever," said Mom.

"No way do you get to stay up later than me," said Stink.

"So you agree?" Judy asked Mom and Dad. "I should get all these freedoms? And a bunch more allowance?"

"We didn't say that," said Dad.

"We'll think it over, honey," said Mom.

"Think it over?" said Judy. Thinking it over was worse than maybe. Thinking it over meant only one thing—N-O.

Then Dad started talking like a sugar packet. "Freedom doesn't come without a price, you know," he told Judy.

"Dad's right," said Mom. "If you want more freedom, you're going to have to earn it—show us you can be more responsible."

Judy looked over her list. "Can I at least have Alien Right Number One? If I didn't have to brush my hair every day, I'd have more time to be responsible."

"Nice try," said Dad.

Parents! Mom and Dad were just like

King George, making up Bad Laws all the time.

"You guys always tell me it's good to stand up for stuff. Speak up for yourself and everything." Judy held up her Declaration. "That's what I just did. But I'm not even one teeny bit more free. That really stinks on ice!"

"Tell you what." Mom looked over the list. "You can have your own washcloth." Dad started to laugh but turned it into a cough.

"Tori has her own phone AND her own bathroom. And pounds of allowance. She can buy all the Bonjour Bunny stuff she wants, without even asking. And she drinks tea. And wakes herself up with her own alarm clock. And she has sleepovers in her flat that's not a tire."

"We're not talking about Tori," said Mom. "We're talking about you."

Crumb cakes! She, Judy Moody, did not have any new freedoms at all. Not one single alien right from her list. All she had was a lousy washcloth.

"ROAR!" said Judy.

"If you don't want the washcloth, I'll take it," said Stink.

Huzzah!

Judy went to bed her same old un-free self. But the next morning, she decided Mom and Dad and the world would see a brand-new Judy Moody. A free and independent Judy. A more responsible Judy. Even on a school day.

Judy started by getting out of bed (without an alarm clock) before her mom had to shake her awake.

Next, she brushed her teeth without

complaining. Mom had set out a new blue washcloth—a plain old boring blue wash-cloth, but it was just for her. Judy wrote *Bonjour Bunny* on it, and made the capital *B*s into funny bunny ears.

Then Judy did something she had not done for three days. She brushed her hair (and put on her Bonjour Bunny headband from Tori.) A responsible person did not have bird's-nest hair.

Then Judy did something she had not done for three weeks. She made her bed. A grown-up, independent person did not have a bed that looked like a yard sale.

❀   ❀   ❀

On the bus, Judy told Rocky about the star-spangled bananas at the Giant Milk Bottle and the Sugar Packet Girl named Tori and about throwing tea off the Tea Party Ship. She could not wait to tell her teacher and her whole class.

"What are you going to tell your class about Boston?" she asked Stink.

"The musical toilet," said Stink. "What else?"

When Judy got to school, she told Mr. Todd and the whole class all about Boston. "We went on the Freedom Trail and it was so NOT boring, and it's okay I missed my spelling test because I learned stuff there, too, like about Mr. Ben Famous Franklin and Paul Revere and—"

"Judy! Take a breath!" said Mr. Todd. "We're glad to have you back."

Judy showed them her *Paul Revere's Ride* flip book and explained all about tea and taxes to the class.

"My mom drinks tea, and she's not a traitor," said Rocky.

"I went to Boston once to visit my grandpa," said Jessica Finch.

"Sounds like you had quite an educational trip, Judy," said Mr. Todd. "Thanks for sharing with us. Maybe I'll read your book aloud in our reading circle today.

First, let's take out our math facts from yesterday."

Judy multiplied 28 x 6, 7, 8, 9, and 10 until she thought her eyes would pop. At last, Mr. Todd announced it was reading-circle time.

"Today I'll be reading a poem Judy brought to share with us from her trip to Boston, called *Paul Revere's Ride*. This poem tells a story."

"I saw his house and his real wallpaper and his false teeth and everything!" said Judy.

"This was my favorite poem when I was a boy," Mr. Todd continued. "In school, we had to memorize it and recite it by heart.

It's by a man named Henry Wadsworth Longfellow. The poem tells about three men and their famous midnight ride during the American Revolution. One of those men was Paul Revere."

Judy raised her hand. "And one was a doctor!" she told the class.

"Shh!" said Jessica Finch.

Mr. Todd lowered his voice to a whisper. Class 3T got super quiet.

"'Listen, my children, and you shall hear
Of the midnight ride of Paul Revere. . . .'"

The poem told all about how Paul Revere rode on horseback through the night to warn each farm and town that the British were coming.

Judy raised her hand again. "Mr. Todd, Mr. Todd! I saw Ye Olde Church where they hung the lanterns! For real! You know how it says, 'One if by land, two if by sea'? Paul Revere said to light one lantern if the British were sneaking in by land, two if they were coming across the water."

"Did that guy really ride his horse and do all that stuff?" asked Jessica Finch. "Because I never even heard about it the whole time I was in Boston."

"It's true," said Mr. Todd. "Paul Revere warned two very important people, Sam Adams and John Hancock, to flee. But before he could warn everybody, he was stopped by the British and his horse was taken."

"But the doctor escaped and warned everybody!" said Judy.

"That's right," said Mr. Todd. "You know, there's also a girl who had a famous ride just like Paul Revere. Her name was Sybil Ludington."

Star-spangled bananas! A Girl Paul Revere! Judy Moody could not believe her Bonjour Bunny ears.

"They don't often tell about her in the history books," said Mr. Todd, "but we have a book about her in our classroom library."

"Huzzah!" said Judy Moody.

"Huh?" asked Frank.

"It's Revolutionary for YIPPEE!" Judy said.

The UN-Freedom Trail

She, Judy Moody, was the luckiest kid in Class 3T. Mr. Todd let her take the Girl Paul Revere book home. Judy read it to Rocky on the bus. She read it to Mouse the cat. She read it to Jaws the Venus flytrap.

Sybil Ludington lived in New York, and her dad needed someone to ride a horse through the dark, scary forest to warn everybody that the British were burning down a nearby town. Sybil was brave and told her dad she could do it. She stayed up late past midnight and rode off into the dark all by herself. Sybil Ludington sure was grown-up and responsible. She showed tons of independence.

Judy would be just like Sybil Ludington. Responsible. Independent. All she had to do was prove it to Mom and Dad. There was only one problem.

She, Judy Moodington, did not have a horse.

And she would never in a million years be allowed to stay up past midnight.

Crumb cakes! She'd just have to be responsible right here in her very own house, 117 Croaker Road. Starting N-O-W.

Judy went from room to room all over the upstairs. She picked stuff up, put stuff away, hid stuff in the closet. Downstairs, she picked up one cat-hair fur ball, two giant lint balls, her basketball, Stink's soccer ball, and Mouse's jingle ball.

Being responsible sure made a person hungry.

Judy stopped to eat some peanut butter with a spoon (not her finger!) out of the jar. She stopped to feed Mouse (not peanut butter) and empty out the litter box (P.U!). She stopped to do some homework (without one single peanut-butter fingerprint!).

Mom and Dad were always bugging her to be nice to Stink, so she went up to his room to be nice. She looked on his desk. She looked under his bed.

"What are you looking for?" asked Stink.

"I'm looking for something nice to say," said Judy. "I like that ant farm poster on your wall."

"You gave it to me," said Stink.

"Well, um . . . your hair looks good."

"Did you put something in my hair?" Stink shook his head. "Eeww, get it out!"

"Stink! Nothing's in your hair. Not even a spider."

Stink plucked at his hair like a dog with fleas.

"I said *not even*! I was just trying to be nice."

Judy never knew independent people had to be so nice. And so clean. But wouldn't Mom and Dad be surprised when they saw all the stuff she could do on her own? Without anybody telling her she had to. She, Judy Moody, would be Independent-with-a-capital-*I*. Just like Sybil Ludington. For sure and absolute positive.

Judy traced her feet onto red construction paper. *Snip, snip, snip!* She made a trail of red footprints all through the house. Not a messy, drop-your-stuff-everywhere trail. An independent, show-how-responsible-you-are trail. She even made signs for each stop along the way, just like the real Freedom Trail.

Now all she had to do was find Mom and Dad and Stink.

⊚ ⊚ ⊚

"The trail starts here," said Judy. She pointed to the sign in front of a wilted, half-dead plant: YE OLDE LIBERTY TREE.

"First I'll make a speech at Ye Olde Liberty Tree. Hear ye! Hear ye!" called Judy, jingling Mouse again. "Give me liberty or give me more allowance!" Mom and Dad laughed. Stink snorted.

"Listen, ye olde trail people. I'm Judy. I'll be your tour guide. Follow the red footprints to freedom!" Judy led her family from room to room.

On the dining room table, it said, JUDY MOODY DID HOMEWORK HERE.

"I do my homework there every day," said Stink. Judy gave him ye olde hairy eyeball.

On the kitchen floor, Judy pointed to a sign that said, JUDY MOODY FED MOUSE HERE.

"Isn't that one of your chores already?" asked Dad.

"Yes," said Judy. "But nobody had to remind me to do it."

She pointed to the kitchen table: JUDY MOODY ATE PEANUT BUTTER HERE.

"I don't get it," said Stink.

"I ate it with a spoon, not my fingers, and I didn't eat any in my room or get it on stuff," said Judy.

Judy opened the door to the laundry room: JUDY MOODY PICKED UP LINT BALLS HERE. She opened the door to the downstairs bathroom: JUDY MOODY WASHED THE SOAP HERE.

"I hate the dope who thought up soap," Stink recited, cracking himself up. "I wish he'd eat it. I repeat it. Eat it."

Stink was not helping on the trail to freedom one bit. "Stink, stop saying stuff," said Judy.

"It's a free country," said Stink.

They followed the red footprints up the stairs to Judy's room. A sign on the bottom bunk said, JUDY MOODY MADE THE BED HERE. One on the top bunk said, PRIVATE! DON'T LOOK UP HERE.

"What are all those lumps up there?" asked Stink.

"Next stop, Stink's room," said the tour guide. His door had a sign taped to it: JUDY MOODY WAS NICE TO STINK HERE.

"Were not!" said Stink.

"Was too!" said Judy.

"Ha!" said Stink. "You told me I had a spider in my hair!"

"Last but not least, the big bathroom!" said Judy. JUDY MOODY PICKED UP THE P.U. TOWELS HERE.

"So what do you think?" Judy asked. "Wasn't I super-duper, Sybil-Ludington responsible?"

"This is great, honey. Everything looks

really good," said Dad. "You're starting to show us that you can be responsible and do things independently."

"It's nice when we don't have to tell you all the time," said Mom.

"So I can have more freedoms now? Like not brushing my hair all the time? And staying up later than Stink?"

"I want freedoms, too!" said Stink. "Chocolate milk for breakfast!"

"We're proud of you, Judy," Mom said. "But these are all things we want you to do anyway."

"You already get an allowance for doing these things," said Dad.

Tarnation! Judy was in a nark again. The narkiest.

The Freedom Trail was not free at all. The UN-Freedom Trail.

She, Judy Moody, picked up P.U. towels and washed soap and ate peanut-butter-not-with-her-fingers for nothing.

"It's just plain ye olde not fair!" she cried.

The Boston Tub Party

When Judy got home from school the next day, there was a mysterious package waiting for her.

"It has queens on it!" said Stink.

"It's from Tori!" Judy tore off the tape. "Sugar packets! For my collection!" There were clipper ships and castles, knights and queens. Even famous London stuff like Big Ben and the World's Largest Ferris Wheel, the London Eye.

"Rare!" said Judy. "Here's one in French. *'Je vois le chat.'* Stink, can you read it?"

Stink squinted at the sugar packet. "I think it says, 'Your head is toast.'"

"Does not!" said Judy. "Give it!" She read the back. "It says, 'I see the cat.'"

Judy found some that Tori had made herself, with funny British sayings like nuddy pants and stuff.

Amazed = gobsmacked
Throw up = pavement pizza
Crazy = barmy, off your trolley

"Can I have the pavement pizza one?" asked Stink.

"You're off your trolley, Stink."

"When was I *on* my trolley?" he asked.

Judy read the Bonjour Bunny postcard.

Bonjour, Judy!
Hope you like the
sugar packets for
your collection—
all the way from
England! Don't
drink too much tea!
Cheerio!
YNFFE, Tori xox
(Your New friend from England)

POST

Judy Moody
U. S. A.

"There's a bunch of tea bags here, too. Real English tea, like at the Boston Tea Party," Judy said. "Tori's barmy if she thinks I'm even allowed to drink all this tea."

"Only traitors drink tea from England," said Stink.

"I'll be a traitor," said Mom. "I'd love to try some English tea." She selected one in shiny blue foil and headed for the kitchen.

Wait just a Yankee-Doodle minute! Judy had a not-so-barmy, off-your-trolley idea. She was gobsmacked that she hadn't thought of it before.

Since Mom and Dad would not let her have more freedoms, she would rise up and protest. Brilliant!

@   @   @

The next day at school, Judy passed notes to Rocky and Frank:

On Saturday, Rocky and Frank rang the Moodys' doorbell at exactly two minutes after twelve. Judy and Stink both ran for the door. Stink got there first. "It's not a Toad Pee Club meeting!" he blurted. "Judy lied. It's a *Tea Party* Club!"

"No way," said Frank.

"I'm not drinking any old tea with a bunch of dolls," said Rocky.

"Not that kind of tea party," said Judy, dragging them up to the bathroom. "C'mon. It'll be fun. Ben Franklin's honor!"

"I see tea bags," said Frank. "And a teapot."

"This is boring," said Rocky.

"Look! It's the talking teapot!" said

Stink. "From when Judy was little." He pressed a button.

"I'm a little teapot," the teapot sang, "short . . . like . . . Stink."

"Did it just say 'short like Stink'?" Frank asked. He cracked up.

"No—it said 'short and stout,'" said Stink. "The batteries are running out!"

"Forget about the teapot," said Judy. "This is a *Boston* Tea Party." Judy explained about the real Boston Tea Party. "It's a protest! Right here. In the bathtub!"

"What's a protest?" asked Frank.

"You get to yell about stuff that's not fair," said Judy.

"Then I protest having a tea party," said Rocky.

"And you get to dump tea in the bathtub," said Stink.

"The Boston *Tub* Party!" said Judy.

"The Wig Guy said everybody dressed up and painted their faces so nobody would know who they were," said Stink.

"Way cool," said Frank.

Stink got a bunch of funny hats from his room. "I call the tricorn hat!" said Rocky.

"I have face paints," said Judy.

Frank painted a not-cracked Liberty Bell on her cheek.

"Did you know they rang the Liberty Bell when they first read the Declaration of Independence?" Judy told Frank.

Stink got a mustache. Rocky got a beard. And Frank got a Frankenstein scar.

Judy filled the tub with hot water. "Okay, everybody think about stuff that's not fair. Ready? Now, on the count of three, throw your tea into the tub. One, two . . . WAIT!"

"What's wrong?" asked Frank.

"It has to be dark. The real Tea Party was after dark." She turned out the big light, and the night-light flickered on.

"We can pretend it's the moon," said Rocky. "At midnight."

"THREE!" called Frank. He took the lid off the pot and dumped the tea into the tub. Rocky and Judy ripped open boxes of tea and tea-bag wrappers.

"Hey, let me!" said Stink. "You guys are hogging."

"Stink, you be on the lookout. Blink the light if you hear Dad coming. One if by stairs, two if by hallway."

Stink stood by the door. "You forgot to hoot and holler and yell not-fair stuff," said Stink.

Everybody started yelling and throwing tea bags into the bathtub.

"No more homework!" said Rocky.

"More allowance!" said Judy.

"More chocolate milk!" said Stink.

"No baby-sitting! No garbage patrol!" said Frank.

Stink took off his shoes and socks, hopped right into the tub, and started acting like a teapot. He made one arm into a handle and one into a spout.

"I'm a little teapot, short and stout," he sang. "When I get all steamed up, hear me shout, 'Give me chocolate milk or give me death!'" He sprayed water out of his mouth.

"Ooh, you spit on me," said Rocky.

"You're getting us all wet!" cried Frank.

Judy thought she heard footsteps on the stairs. "The British are coming! The British are coming!" she warned.

A voice, a deep voice, a *Dad* voice, said, "Hey, what's all the—"

"Abandon ship! Abandon ship!" Judy cried.

"What in the world is going on up here?" asked Dad, opening the bathroom door. "Sounds like an elephant in the bath-tub." He turned on the lights.

Water dripped from the walls like a rain forest. The floor was flooded with giant brown puddles. Stink drip-drip-dripped like a short and stout wet mop.

The tub water was a brown sea of murky, ucky, yucky tea. Tea bags bobbed up and down on the tiny bathtub waves. The Boston Mud Party.

"Judy?" asked Dad. "Stink?"

Stink pointed to Judy. "It was her idea!"

"We were having a Boston Tea Party," said Judy.

"Judy," said Dad. "Just a few days ago, you were showing off this *clean* bathroom."

"But Dad! It's a protest! For more freedoms."

"A mess this size sure isn't going to get you more allowance . . . or your own bathroom."

"Pretend this is Boston Harbor. We were just making history come alive. Like homework."

"Sorry. This harbor's closed. Rocky, Frank, it's time for you boys to go home. Judy, no more friends over for one week. And you'd better get this mess cleaned up before Mom gets home. You too, Stink."

"But I don't even want independence!" said Stink. "Just more chocolate milk."

"The Patriots swept up after they threw tea in the harbor," Dad said.

No friends for one week! This was just
like what the British did to the Americans—
one of those Bad Laws they called the
In-tol-er-able Acts. Dad was closing down
the tub just like the Big Meanies closed
down the harbor after the real Tea Party!

Judy felt like stamping her feet (the Stamp Act). She felt like throwing sugar packets (the Sugar Act). She felt like declaring independence *on the wall* (in permanent marker)!

But just like all the Bad Laws in the world did not stop the Patriots, the Clean-the-Bathroom-Again Law and No-Friends-for-One-Week Law would not stop her. And they would not, could not, put her in a nark. They were just bumps in the road on the Judy Moody March to Freedom.

She, Judy Moody, would live by a Not-Bad Law, the Law of the Sugar Packet: *If at first you don't succeed, try, try again.*

Sybil La-Dee-Da

When Judy got out of bed on Monday morning, she did not stamp one foot. She did not throw one sugar packet. Instead, she quietly-and-to-herself declared independence from brushing her teeth and taking a shower. She did not want to mess up the bathroom again. EVER.

Her makeup book report from when she was in Boston was due today. A makeup book report was NOT going to put her in a bad mood. Even if she had waited till the last minute. Judy decided right then and there to make this her best-ever book report. That's what a responsible person would do.

She dressed up in her pilgrim costume— the one Grandma Lou had made for Halloween. *Ye olde pilgrimme costoom* had an apron and made Judy look just like a girl from the American Revolution. Judy wore regular-not-loony pants underneath the skirt for bloomers. And she made thirteen curls in her hair—one for each of the thirteen colonies.

"Who are you? Heidi?" Stink asked at breakfast.

"None of your beeswax," said Judy.

"Are you a nurse?"

"N-O!" said Judy.

"Hey, I know. You're Priscilla Somebody! Like a pilgrim?"

"No, I'm Revolutionary. The Girl Paul Revere. For my book report today."

"Oh. So you're that Sybil La-Dee-Da?"

It sure was hard to declare independence from bad moods when Stink was around.

"Bye, Mom. Bye, Dad," Judy called on her way out the door.

"Hey, wait for me!" Stink yelled.

"Sorry! I'm riding my faster-than-lightning bike to the bus stop!" Judy yelled back. And she was off.

Right before the end of the school day, it was time for Judy's book report. She asked Frank Pearl to help her. They stood up in front of the class.

"Mr. Todd? I have a different kind of book report. It's acted out. Like a play."

"Cool!" said Rocky.

"The book I read is called *Sybil: The Female Paul Revere*," Judy told her class. "It's about the Girl Paul Revere. And this," she said, pointing to Frank, "is the Boy Paul Revere. Frank—I mean Paul—is helping me, Sybil Ludington."

Judy started with a poem: "'Listen, my children, and you shall hear / Of a girl who rode way farther than Paul Revere.'"

SYBIL: Hey, Paul Revere? Why are you
so famous?

PAUL: Because, Sybil Ludington, I rode
my horse all night. I warned everybody the British were coming.

SYBIL: I did, too. My horse is named Star.
It was dark. I was scared. It rained
all night. I was brave. It was muddy.

PAUL: It wasn't muddy when I rode.

SYBIL: Well, la-dee-da.

"No fair! It doesn't say that here!" said
Frank.

"I just added it," said Judy. "Keep reading."

PAUL: I'm forty years old and I rode
sixteen miles.

SYBIL: I'm only sixteen and I rode almost
forty miles.

PAUL: I made it to Lexington to warn Sam Adams and John Hancock.

SYBIL: Hey, Paul? Weren't you caught by the British?

PAUL: At first I wasn't. Then I was.

SYBIL: Didn't Mr. Todd say they took your horse?

PAUL: Yes.

SYBIL: Aha! So you got caught and didn't finish warning everybody. I, Sybil Ludington, DIDN'T get caught, and I warned everybody. I yelled, 'Stop the British. Mustard at Ludingtons!' All the British had to go back on their ships. Then everybody came to my house for hot dogs (with mustard). Even Mr. George Famous Washington. The end.

"Did Sybil What's-Her-Face really eat hot dogs?" asked Jessica Finch.

"She ate mustard," said Judy. "Ketchup wasn't invented yet."

Mr. Todd chuckled. "Actually, the word is *muster*, not *mustard*. When Sybil rode her horse to warn everybody, she called them to muster, which means to get together."

"The other parts were all true," said Judy. "I give this book five *really*s. As in really, really, really, really, really good. It was so good, I stayed inside for recess to read it. It was so good, I read it to my cat and my Venus flytrap!"

"Thank you, Judy," said Mr. Todd. "Sounds like Sybil Ludington really inspired you."

"Everybody should know about the Girl Paul Revere. Most people never heard of her, because for some barmy reason they forgot to put girls in history books. I wouldn't even know about her if you hadn't told me."

"Maybe some others will want to read the book now," said Mr. Todd.

"Sybil Ludington should be in our social studies book for everybody to read about. Girls should get to be in history books, too, you know. Especially girls who did independent stuff, don't you think?"

"Yes, yes, I do," said Mr. Todd.

"Girls rule!" all the girls shouted.

"Huzzah!" said Judy.

The Declaration of UN-Independence

On the bus ride home, Rocky told Judy how much he liked her book report. "When I first saw you looking like a pilgrim, I was sure it would be boring. But it was WAY not boring."

"Thanks," said Judy. "I hope I get a way good grade and it shows my Mom and Dad how grown-up and responsible I am."

"Just think," Rocky said, "how super scary it must have been when Sybil rode through the woods . . . and it was dark and robbers were all around."

"But she had to stop the British from burning down the whole town of Danbury!"

"Yeah. But if she got caught, the bad guys might think she was a spy!" Rocky said.

Judy and Rocky talked about Sybil all the way home.

When they got off the bus, Judy started walking, then said, "Oops, I almost forgot. I rode my bike to the bus stop today."

"Okay. See ya!" called Rocky as he loped off toward his house. Judy unlocked her bike. Behind her, the doors of the bus hissed and closed, and the brakes squeaked as it pulled away from the curb.

Wait . . . something was not right.

Stink?

STINK!

Stink did not get off the bus! Stink had never NOT gotten off the bus before.

☻   ☻   ☻

Judy could not think. She was sure she'd seen him get ON the bus. Should she yell for help? Race home and get Mom?

"HEY!" yelled Judy. "Mr. Bus Driver! HEY!" she shouted. The bus was already driving off down the street.

WWBFD? What would Ben Franklin do? Go to bed early? Save a penny? Judy did not think sugar packet sayings could help her now.

There was only one thing to do. Chase the bus!

Mom would worry if she didn't come right home, but there was no time to go tell her. Not when her brother was being kidnapped by a runaway bus.

She, Judy Moody, had to get her brother back. No matter how stinky he was, he was still her brother.

Judy hitched up her pilgrim skirt and

hopped on her bike. She pedaled hard. She pedaled fast. She rode like the wind. She rode like Sybil on Star. She chased that bus down the street and around the corner and up the hill and down the hill.

Cars whizzed by. *Whoosh!* Dirt flew in her face. She swerved to miss a big hole in the road. What if she fell off her bike and broke her head?

Judy kept riding. She tooted her horn. She yelled, "HEY! Mr. Bus! My brother's on there. GIVE! ME! BACK! MY! BROTHER!"

The bus kept going.

A dog barked at her. What if a big meany dog got loose and chased her? What if she got bitten by a wild dog? A wild dog with RABIES?

Judy pedaled faster. Wind flapped her skirt and whipped her thirteen curls every which way. A big green garbage truck screamed by, way too close. Judy's wheels wobbled. Her handlebars shook. The truck honked at her, *wooomp*, deep like a foghorn. Her heart pounded.

What if she got run over by a P.U. garbage truck?

She rode her bike all the way to Bacon Avenue. Traffic! Cars! Trucks! Red lights!

Then she saw it. The bus! The school bus, bright as a big cheese in the middle of the road. It had crossed the intersection and was heading up the hill on the other side of Third Street.

Mom and Dad would FREAK if she crossed the busy street in the middle of traffic by herself. But they might freak more if she came home late . . . without Stink!

WWSLD? What would Sybil Ludington do? Sybil would think for herself. Be independent. Be brave.

Judy hopped off and wheeled her bike to the crosswalk. She waited for the Big Red Hand on the sign to change to the Big Bright Walking Man. "Hurry up!" Judy yelled at the light. "The bus is getting away!"

Finally, the light changed. She looked both ways, took a deep breath, and crossed the street safely.

Judy hopped back on her bike and zoomed up the hill. Puff, puff, puff.

Judy huffed and puffed until she caught up with the bus. "Stink!" she shouted, biking on the sidewalk, right alongside the bus. The bus driver looked over. Judy pointed to the back of the bus. "My brother!"

At last! The bus stopped to let some kids off. The door rattled open. "My little brother . . . *puff, puff* . . . is . . . *puff, puff* . . . on that bus!" Judy yelled.

Stink was already rushing up to the front of the bus. "I fell asleep!" he told Judy. "And then I woke up and you were gone and I didn't know where I was! I was so scared."

"It's okay," said Judy. "I chased you and I found you and you're safe now." Stink clutched her shirtsleeve and wouldn't let go.

"Thank you," she said to the driver. "Thanks for stopping. C'mon, Stinker. Let's go home."

@ @ @

When Judy and Stink got home—over an hour late—Mom was mad-with-a-capital-*M*. "I thought I asked you to come straight home after school," Mom said. "You scared me half to death!" She said she was scared and worried sick, but she did not look sick. Just M-A-D.

She did not even give Judy a chance to explain. "Judy, you know better than this. Go to your room. Now!"

"Stink should go to his room, too. He's the one who fell asleep and—"

Mom's lips turned into a thin white line. "I don't want to hear it!" said Mom. She pointed upstairs.

Judy slunk up to her room, crawled into bed, and got under her baby quilt. She, Judy Moody, Friend of Sybil in History, was in trouble again. Trouble with a capital *T*. Worse than the Boston Tub Party.

Grownups! They sure acted like they wanted you to be all independent, but as soon as you were, they went and changed their minds. Independence. HA! All it did was get her in trouble.

Maybe if Judy just declared UN-independence, everything would go back

to the way it was. At least she wouldn't have to clean up so much. And get run over by P.U. garbage trucks while chasing runaway buses.

Judy tried to do her homework, but all the spelling words looked like scrambled eggs. She tried chewing gum for her ABC collection, but all it did was stick to her teeth. She tried starting a scrapbook of her trip to Boston, but even the Declaration of Independence looked sad.

To cheer herself up, Judy wrote a post-card to Tori:

Dear Tori,
Thanks for the tea (and sugar packets). They're my fave! I hAd a tea Party and got in big trouble! I chased the school bus (to get my brother) and got in BIGGER trouble. I hAve a question.

Victoria MulQueeny
4 Brampton Grove
Harrow, Middlesex
ENGLAND

How do you...
1) stay out of trouble
2) get to do all that grown-up stuff?
Hurry up and write back! I'm going DaRmy!

Cheerios! YNPPFA (Your New Pen Pal from America),

⊚ * ⊚ * Judy Moody

Judy tiptoed to the top of the stairs to see if she could hear anything. Mom was talking to Stink. Traitor! He was probably blaming the whole thing on her. Redcoat!

Judy climbed back up to her top bunk. "Here, Mouse," called Judy. At least her cat wasn't mad at her. At least her cat was not a traitor.

Mouse hid under the bottom bunk. "Here, Mousie, Mousie." Mouse still did not budge. Even her cat was declaring independence.

Judy's whole room was in a mood. For sure and absolute positive.

After about a hundred years, Stink rattled the doorknob. "Open up!"

"Go away, Stink," Judy told him.

"Open up, honey." That did not sound like Stink. That sounded like Mom. Nice Mom, not Will-You-Ever-Learn Mom.

"We just want to talk to you, Judy." That sounded like Dad. Kind Dad, not You-Are-in-Big-Trouble Dad.

"Am I in big trouble?" Judy asked the door. "Because if I am, then I declare UN-independence. I promise I will NOT make my bed or do my homework or be nice to Stink. And I will definitely not rescue him anymore. EVER!"

"Judy, open the door so we can talk about this," said Dad.

Judy opened the door. Mom rushed to

hug her. Dad ruffled Judy's hair and kissed the top of her head.

"Stink told us what happened," said Dad. "That was a very brave thing you did."

"It was?"

"I'm sorry, honey," said Mom. "It gave me quite a scare when you two didn't come right home, so I didn't even stop to listen. You had a hard choice to make, and you really used some good, independent thinking."

"I did?"

"You sure did," said Dad.

"I was scared, too," said Judy. "I thought a big meany dog might bite me or a

garbage truck might run me over or I'd fall and break my head or something. I just kept thinking about Sybil Ludington and how she was scared, too."

"We're very proud of you, Sybil," Dad said. "I mean Judy."

"Proud enough to give me more allowance and stuff?"

"Dad and I will talk things over," said Mom. "Maybe you *are* ready for a little more independence."

She, Judy Moodington, was not in big-or-little-*T* trouble. And she showed independent thinking. Just like Sybil Ludington.

Star-spangled bananas!

Yankee Doodle Dandy

After all the excitement, Judy was feeling much too independent to do homework. She got out her Judy Moody Declaration of Independence. This was going straight into her scrapbook.

Judy climbed up to her top bunk. She spread out all the stuff from her trip to Boston. In her scrapbook, she pasted, taped, glue-sticked, or Band-Aided all her souvenirs from Boston.

Last but not least, she turned the page and pasted sugar packets with Ben Franklin sayings onto the page. And she made up a new one:

If at first your brother falls asleep on the bus, ride, ride like Sybil and chase after him.

❧   ❧   ❧

The next day, the story of the not-so-midnight ride of Judy Moody was all over Virginia Dare School.

Listen, my children, and you shall hear
How Judy Moody rode like Sybil and
Paul Revere.

Every time Stink told the story, it got a little wilder. Some heard she was chased by wild wolves. Some heard she was kidnapped by a garbage truck. Some heard she fell and broke her leg but kept on riding.

Stink even made Judy a gold medal with a blue ribbon.

☙   ☙   ☙

After dinner that night, Judy climbed up to the top bunk to paste the ribbon into her scrapbook.

The scrapbook was not there! As in G-O-N-E, gone!

She looked under her reading pillow. She looked under lumps of covers and heaps of stuffed animals. She looked under Mouse.

Judy looked all around her room. The

scrapbook was missing. The scrapbook was stolen! By Number One Scrapbook Thief, right here in the Moody house.

"Stink!" Judy ran into his room. "I did not say you could take my scrapbook. Give it!"

"I didn't take your scrapbook," said Stink.

"After I saved your life and everything!" said Judy. "Robber! Stealer! Scrapbook-napper!"

"Am not! I swear on Toady's life I didn't take it."

"If you didn't take it, and I didn't lose it, that leaves Mouse. And Mouse can't read!"

"Maybe Mom and Dad took it," Stink said. "Let's go ask."

"Let's go *spy*," said Judy.

Judy and Stink tiptoed down the stairs without too many creaks. They slid across the floor without too many squeaks. They slunk past the living room, past the kitchen, to Mom's office.

"Stink, you hold the flashlight. I'll look around." She pawed through the trash. She searched on top of the file cabinet and in the bookshelves.

"Uh-oh!" Stink said. "Check it out!" A message was flashing across Mom's computer screen. It said:

```
JUDY AND STINK,
IF YOU ARE READING THIS, I
KNOW YOU'RE IN HERE.
READ THIS NOTE:
XLOW UVVG ZIV MLG HDVVG.
```

"How can we read it? It's in Russian," Stink said, shining the light on the screen.

"It's not Russian," said Judy. "It's secret code. SPY code. It looks just like Dr. Church's secret code in Dad's Freedom Trail book from Boston. Rare!"

"The spy guy? Sweet! We can be code busters, just like him."

"Yep." Judy ran and got her book. She looked it up in the back. "The code is A=Z, B=Y, and C=X. All you have to do is use the alphabet backward."

They looked at the letters again: XLOW UVVG ZIV MLG HDVVG. Judy figured it out. "COLD FEET ARE NOT SWEET. Hmm. It's some sort of clue. Not sweet . . . not sweet."

"How about the cookie jar?" Stink asked.

"It says NOT sweet, Stink."

"How about socks? Socks aren't sweet. And they help cold feet."

"Brilliant!" Judy and Stink dashed upstairs, where Judy rummaged through her sock drawer. Sure enough, there was another clue sticking out of her Screamin' Mimi's ice-cream socks.

"It's like a treasure hunt." She opened the note and it read: QFWB GRNVH GDL, YLGS ZIV BLF. She took out her pencil and figured it out in her notebook. "This one says, JUDY TIMES TWO, BOTH ARE YOU."

They thought about it for a long time. They were both stumped. Then Judy got a brainstorm! "There's only one me," said Judy.

"You can say that again," said Stink.

"Unless . . . I look in a mirror!" Judy and Stink raced for the bathroom. On the bathroom mirror, a message was written in soap crayons: Z SLFHV ULI NLFHV

Stink helped Judy work out the code. "A HOUSE FOR MOUSE!" yelled Judy.

"That doesn't make sense," said Stink.

"Think," said Judy. "What else could be a house for Mouse?"

"Under your bed?" asked Stink. "Or your top bunk?"

"I looked there," said Judy. "Wait! I got it! Where is Mouse whenever we can't find her?"

"The dirty-laundry basket!" said Stink. He ran downstairs after his sister. Judy raced over to the pile of laundry on the washer and dug around. "Found it!" she said, holding up her scrapbook.

They flipped through pages of pictures and pebbles, pressed leaves and pencil rubbings, tea bags and sugar packets and Band-Aids, her Declaration of Independence, the postcard from Tori.

She flipped to the last page. She, Judy Moody, was gobsmacked! Glued to the page was a fancy certificate on old-timey paper that looked like parchment.

Hear ye! Hear ye! Judy Moody has hereby . . .
Made her bed every day
Brushed her hair (almost) every day
Done her homework without being asked
Been nice to Stink
Inspired others with her bravery and
courage on her famous ride

. . . which demonstrates independent thinking.
We, the undersigned (Mom and Dad), hereby
grant Judy Moody a 25¢ raise in her allowance,
effective now.
Signed,
Kate "Betsy Ross" Moody (aka Mom)
Richard "John Hancock" Moody (aka Dad)

Taped to the same page was a shiny
new quarter.

"Holy macaroni!" said Judy. "Look! A
Maine quarter with a lighthouse! Now I

have liberty AND the purse of happiness."

"And with more allowance, you can pay me back a lot faster!" said Stink.

"Wait till I write to Tori and tell her. My Declaration of Independence really worked!"

"Except for the getting your own bathroom thing."

Judy Moody hugged her scrapbook, then Stink. She found Mom and Dad and hugged them, too. She even kissed Mouse on her wet pink nose.

"Independence doesn't end here," said Mom. "We're going to expect you to keep being responsible."

"And, of course, you still always have to do your homework," Dad told her.

"And be nice to me!" said Stink.

"Maybe I could also stay up a teeny-weeny bit late? Just for tonight?" asked Judy. "On account of how independent I am now and how I'm not going to be treated like a baby anymore and stuff."

"Fifteen minutes," said Dad.

"And just for tonight," said Mom.

Fifteen whole minutes!

"No fair!" said Stink. "Then I'm declaring independence from brushing my teeth! Give me liberty or give me bad breath!"

"One independent kid is enough for now," said Mom. Dad laughed.

That night, in those fifteen minutes, Judy ate a snack of grapes and goldfish (the crackers!). She brushed her teeth with red, white, and blue toothpaste and washed her face with her very own (Bonjour Bunny) washcloth. She read a whole chapter of her *Ramona the Brave* library book. After only twelve and a half minutes, she couldn't even stay awake anymore. She climbed the ladder to her top bunk.

"Lights out!" said Mom. "Good night, sweetie." Dad blew her a kiss.

After Mom and Dad pulled the door almost-shut, Judy lay on her top bunk and gazed up at the night-sky ceiling full of glow-in-the-dark stars.

Star-spangled bananas! She, Judy Moody, was Independent-with-a-capital-*I*. As independent as Ben Franklin. John

Hancock. Paul Revere. As independent as Sybil Ludington on her midnight ride.

Being independent was brilliant! The bee's knees. And staying up late was Yankee Doodle Dandy.

Judy was getting sleepy. So sleepy. But just before she drifted off, she took out her flashlight pen and wrote something on the wall, in permanent marker, right next to her pillow:

JUDY MOODY SLEPT HERE.

Judy Moody
Slept Here

Megan McDonald ——————

is the award-winning author of the Judy Moody series. She says that most of Judy's stories "grew out of anecdotes about growing up with my four sisters." She confesses, "I *am* Judy Moody. Same-same! In my family of sisters, we're famous for exaggeration. Judy Moody is me . . . exaggerated." Megan McDonald lives with her husband in northern California, with two dogs, two adopted horses, and fifteen wild turkeys.

Peter H. Reynolds ——————

says he felt an immediate connection to Judy Moody because, "having a daughter, I have witnessed firsthand the adventures of a very independent-minded girl." Peter H. Reynolds lives in Massachusetts, just down the street from his twin brother.

Praise for
Judy Moody
Declares Independence

An International Reading Association Children's Choice

"Fans can cheer 'Huzzah! Huzzah!' for Judy as she connects history with her own story."
—*San Francisco Chronicle*

"Judy's petitioning for parental concessions will spark recognition in many readers, and in both McDonald's charismatic narrative and Reynolds's line drawings the characterization of a dauntless, endearingly notional third-grader is as spot-on as ever." —*Booklist*

"Fans get a history lesson delivered with humor, as Judy petitions for her own freedoms—such as more allowance." —*Publishers Weekly*

"A comical, fast-paced story." —*The Horn Book*

Be sure to read Judy's next adventure!

Judy Moody
Around the World in 8½ Days

Megan McDonald   illustrated by Peter H. Reynolds

Hardcover ISBN 978-0-7636-2832-1

And don't forget to check out the adventures of Judy Moody's little brother, Stink!

And coming soon . . .
Stink and the World's Worst Super-Stinky Sneakers

Experience all of Judy Moody's moods!